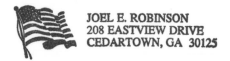 JOEL E. ROBINSON
208 EASTVIEW DRIVE
CEDARTOWN, GA 30125

MUSIC and CRIME

MUSIC
and CRIME

J. R. Creech

G. P. PUTNAM'S SONS
New York

G. P. Putnam's Sons
Publishers Since 1838
200 Madison Avenue
New York, NY 10016

The author gratefully acknowledges permission to quote lyrics from
"Since I Fell For You" by Buddy Johnson © 1948 Warner Bros. Inc.
(Renewed). All rights reserved. Used by permission.

Library of Congress Cataloging-in-Publication Data

Creech, J. R.
  Music and crime.

  I. Title.
ISBN 0-399-13418-2
PS3553.R337M8   1989   813'.54   88-26479

Printed in the United States of America
1 2 3 4 5 6 7 8 9 10

Acknowledgments

I would like to thank everyone
   who ever lent me twenty bucks
An' never got it back—

Three people
  my mother and my father with love,
  and my friend, James H. Morran, the Birdman—

MUSIC and CRIME

1

The saxophone cut into my lap, the weight across my thighs. It never felt so much like a piece of metal, not that I could remember. I fingered it out of habit. Lonnie sat at his little Chinese desk in front of me smoking heroin on a strip of tinfoil. "Chasin' the dragon," he grinned. A pebble of Mexican Tar, black like Lonnie, it disappeared in his fingers as he played with it, then dropped soundlessly on the foil. He smoked it by heating the foil with a lighter from underneath, the tar got hot, smoked so dark it looked purple, it bubbled and began to slide down the foil leaving an oily, brown trail, sticky, and hardened immediately. He sucked the smoke through a tube of rolled paper into his mouth, taking the hits deep in his lungs. His chest pumped and settled. His eyes watered. Whiffs seeped from the corners of Lonnie's fucking grin. He tried to pass the tube to me.

"No, man . . . I'm here to *play*, Lon." I stood up, but didn't go anywhere.

He set the foil down carefully on the table and eased back into his chair; with two fingers he peeked out the window shade, and a bar of sunlight struck his face like a deathray.

"What's the big fuckin' hurry?" he said.

We were in his room over the liquor store Keeber owned, MIDNIGHT LIQUORS 24 HRS. A DAY. And Keeber, maybe his father, maybe not. Any case, we were in his room, the bed with the leopard-skin African quilt-thing that looked like it would smell like dirt, and a wall stacked with electronics, all of it stolen. Sixteen-track, amps, speakers, mini-mixer, two Fender basses and a DX7 keyboard, you name it, a box full of footpedals. We got it from trucks, warehouses, simple cut-the-bottom-out-of-boxes hits that were so quick we never got caught. We stole the stuff to record our music. Lonnie's room had one window and chair, the Chinese table. I don't mean it was a little room; it was big, long like a railroad flat, just empty.

"We haven't done shit," I started on him, but he only smiled back. "All you do is smoke that shit an' thumb a few chords . . . an' run your big Jimi Hendrix dream over an' over."

"Stanley Clark." Lonnie wiped his mouth. "Today, I'm Stanley Clark." He looked up and sighed through his nose at me, like he felt sorry for me. "RayBird . . . FaceMan . . . what'samatta? You *un*easy?"

This was going nowhere. I zipped the sax closed in its snug leather bag and stopped to look at him. "I don't know why I even hang with you, man."

" 'at's easy . . . 'cause you got nobody else."

I chilled at the truth, found my sunglasses and left. In the hallway, behind me, I heard Lonnie's weak words calling out like halfway to dreamland. "Give me an hour'r two . . ." The door closed on a hush.

It was wintertime in L.A. Strange thought even just that, wintertime in L.A. I laughed to myself crossing Main Street; it was the same, every day the same here, the weather was invisible. Every now and then I faced the wind, slapped wide-awake by the cold, every now and then it rained on the ocean and the sunset went yellow and the day sky collapsed. OK, that shit happened in L.A. but it was hardly *weather*. I hated Christmas here and tried to ignore it completely, but there was always the feeling of a chance, like something unexpected and cool might happen. But winter was nothing more than cold sand.

I had three dollars and bought a handful of cheap flowers from the Korean stand on the corner, then went straight for the St. Charles Club on Venice Boulevard.

It was dark with great old "Midnight Train to Georgia" playing on the juke. Jello was behind the bar with one foot up on the speed rack and her elbows spread out on the backbar, leaning into it at an awkward angle, her chest stuck out, showing off. She was the best. Three guys in the bar in the late afternoon and she was teasing them. She pretended not to see me until I sat at my spot on the corner, and when she said, "Ray the Face," it was under her breath and she didn't look at me. I watched her as she mixed a drink, and she liked the feel of me watching, a large, sexual, black woman with a brutally handsome face and quick, nervy, drug eyes. Jello's skin was deep and textured like a piece of unlit night stretched over her, her breasts moved sideways together under a pink cotton shirt. She brought me a beer and saw the flowers laying wounded on the bar. "For me?" she dropped a hand on her throat.

"Sure. Three dollar flowers to get twenty," I said past her, eyeing the guys at the bar.

"Two of those guys are packin'," she said, rolling her hands over on the bar.

"How'd you know?"

"They showed me. RayBird, it's this fuckin' crazy gun law . . . I don't know how they pushed this shit through." She stepped back and her shoes clicked on the drainboards. Jello lifted a thick-barreled pump shotgun from under the bar. It was as long as her arm even with the stock sawed in two. "Look at this goddamn thing I'm draggin' back 'ere."

"You can get licensed for that thing?" I pointed the beer at it.

"Fuckin'-A," she cried. "Hundred an' fifteen dollars is all it takes anymore. Everybody's packin'."

"You're trying to change the subject on me. You think I forgot. The flowers?"

"Goddamnit Ray, this shit can't go on. Pretty soon you'll be wantin' to fuck me too." She went to her purse and pushed a twenty-dollar bill over the counter to me. "I'll spot you the twenty anytime, you good-lookin' whiteass, sexy mothafucker. I'm easy. Doesn't pay to be nice, baby, never did. Yuppies got all the money anyway. You think they give a fuck?" I was fascinated with the water glistening on her pink fingernails as she spoke. I kept my eyes on her hands. Her hands were so strong. "I ought to give you the hundred an' fifteen . . . then you can go get your own . . . much as you want." Jello sat back long enough to light a cigarette in a funny, clear holder. She saw me looking at it. "This thing?" she asked.

"It looks like a toy," I said.

"I'm tryin' to quit . . . this is a water-tip or some shit. I bought the whole program. Tastes like gettin' kissed through a screendoor."

And there was this light rhythm in my head that I wanted to play. I'd heard it in there all day, wasn't sure that it would be there tomorrow. It was only a riff. Jello made me laugh, and suddenly it came back sharper than usual, with an uneasiness I had not linked with it. It was impatient, a challenge.

"You can pay me back on Thursday," Jello was saying.

"Thursday? Why Thursday?"

" 'Cause you're giggin' here, aren't you?"

"I don't know."

"Didn't Lonnie tell you?" She let her face drop, stuck out a few teeth, then her lower lip in thought. "Maybe he didn't get you in yet. Maybe that's why . . . But he said somethin' 'bout you both giggin' with this funky Latin band, Latin All-Stars or some shit. He didn't say nothin'?"

I shook my head.

"He's turnin' into such a little tarbaby."

I said nothing, fighting to hear the music, but it was gone. Then, "Thanks, Jello. You're too good to me."

"You got that right." She pointed to my sax bag as she always did. "An' get yourself a hardcase for that thing. Ray the Face, look at me. As fucked-up as you guys get . . . some day, some day you're gonna ding that baby all up so it won't do you any good. You're gonna smash it."

"Thanks, Jello."

"An' Ray, skip the flowers, Okay? Then you'd have twenty-three bucks." She smiled, mixed three more drinks.

I thought about Jello on the way to the beach as I was sure she was thinking about me. We were two people who would wake up one morning together, roll over and remember the night before, smell the stuffy room and begin to plot an exit. On that day the magic between us would be dead. We would have done it and found out that it wasn't special at all, that it was just like everybody else doing it to each other. It might even be less than special. Imagination was the key, I said to myself, it was so much better than reality, any reality.

At the beach, I squatted to pull off my boots and socks under the palm trees, their spikey green tops unmoving and stiff, surreal. I noticed the dead air. It was wrong; there was always breeze at sunset. Always. I amused myself with the Mexican graffiti sprayed on the sides of the palms, halfway up their trunks and sponged into the tree skin. I touched it, there for life, and waited for the palms to flutter. But no wind.

Here the beach was crowded with the tents of the homeless, the Sand People as we called them, living in their Sandominiums. Walking through I felt like a news spot in a PLO refugee camp anywhere in the sand. It didn't look like California; it was just sand with poles jutting out at straining angles and covers of black plastic or Army surplus green or billowing old parachute material. There were dressers with clothes falling from open drawers, piles of mismatched shoes and stacks of dirty plates, pots and pans tilting in the sand. A scraggily faced kid was washing out his socks in the drinking fountain. There were hundreds of them, each tent different. The Sand People were young, not screaming alcoholic crazy, just jobless, stupid, and unable to live.

And I thought of Allie's girlfriend, a young working paralegal at a big firm, as I waded through the tents toward the surfline, Allies' friend telling us about her Cozumel vacation, sleeping with the windows open to hear the ocean breaking on the shore. ". . . God, it's the only way to sleep . . . with the waves the last thing you hear." She paid $250 a night for it. I looked around. She had a point and didn't know it, but if you had to be a bum, this was a good place to do it.

I was the only tourist on the beach, the only sunset-gazer. I smoked half a joint thinking that it would take me away, out of my own body and thought pattern into something universal and spiritual. Give me a new perspective, a handle, the man with no shoes meeting the man with no feet. But it always came back to the bottom line, and I couldn't shake it. I was a thirty-two-year-old musician and I wasn't making it. How am I going to live?

In time two Sand People came up beside me, a bearded boy in fatigues and a long-haired girl with a homemade

bandaged hand. She held it close to her chest as if it still
hurt. He pointed to the sax case in my lap.

"Hey, play somethin'," he grinned, ". . . play somethin',
man."

2

The boy was still half-asleep. He stood blinking at the bottom of the stairs. To his eyes it was the highest stairway in the world, maybe a thousand wooden steps or even more. He squinted at the bare lightbulb at the top. The landings were crowded with black people laughing and pressing against each other, shaking ice cubes in their glasses. The air was filled with smoke from the cigarettes they held loosely in their fingers, and the lightbulb looked like a yellow sun trying to break through the clouds. The air smelled very bad to him, worse than it smelled in the closet or even under his house with the bugs. His sister squeezed his hand on one side, and his mother stood like a rigid soldier on the other; he looked up at her, but she was staring up at the black people, holding her purse in both hands. He could not understand why she had brought them here.

She had rushed in and taken his sister and the boy from bed, wrapping them in winter coats and fur hats, and put them in the front seat of the car that was already running in the driveway. He had never been awake this late at night before; he had never seen everything so black and quiet and unmoving, and he was asleep before the car reached the end of the block. When his mother woke him for the second time, the car was parked under a giant flashing sign with so many colors he thought he was dreaming again. He watched that sign until his head bent backward from looking at it, as his mother took them inside, sister squeezing his hand like an orange and guiding him across the sidewalk. If he could have put the letters together into words, the sign would have told him they were entering BLUE'S OASIS.

Mother picked him up, pressed him to her chest, his head facing backward over her shoulder, so that as she walked up the long stairway all he could see were the steps falling away behind them, climbing higher and higher. The night people stopped laughing and separated so they could pass, and although they said nothing to his mother or sister, they made funny faces and happy, high voices, shook their heads at him, facing backward. He wanted to watch them but the smoke hurt his eyes and he closed them tight. He became dizzy and confused.

"Put me down, Mama . . . put me down," he cried and kicked. She did just as he threw up on the second landing, splashing vomit on the steps so one black man had to leap back and split his legs to keep from getting it on his shoes.

"Ain't that some shit!" the man exclaimed, brushing himself.

"My God!" answered a woman. "What're you bringin' that child here to get him sick for?" she said to his mother.

"I'm sorry, I'm terribly . . ."

But they continued up. At the top of the stairs they passed through a large open doorway into a room so big and smoke-filled the boy could not see to the other side; people were dancing in the middle all around them, and suddenly he thought of bees, there were so many dancers. Sister was about to cry, but Mother moved them quickly to a table far in the back and the children were saved.

A beautiful black woman with snake bracelets twisting around her arms came up to the table where the boy sat on his mother's lap. She smiled and offered two pieces of candy in the palm of her hand.

"Coupla sweets . . ." she said. The boy thought she was very pretty, her teeth so white and shiny, but he felt his mother's sudden tightening about him, saw her shaking her head no, and the woman walked away. The loud music began playing and he squirmed toward it; his mother took his head in her hands and turned him, pointing at the stage.

"See Daddy . . . see?" she said in his ear.

A blue and white spot exploded at center stage, and his father stood in the middle of it, his feet spread wide apart, his body bent back at the waist, his shoulders rocking easily back and forth as he played. It was a solo, a long crescendo; the other players had stopped. The boy saw the dancing people moving to his father's music, clapping, spinning in small circles, watched him with their mouths open gasping for breath. And he loved his father so much in that moment that he cried because it ever had to end, that the light had to go off, that his father had to sit back down with the others.

But when the music had stopped, he saw him walking to their table, wiping sweat from his face with a white towel. Father lifted his sister first and hugged her, so the boy stretched his arms out too, across the table and Father lifted his children, one in each arm. They sat, the girl with her dad, the boy on his mother's lap. The beautiful black woman brought him a drink, patted his shoulder. "Nice set, Jimmy, nice," she said softly.

"Daddy . . . give me an ice cube," Sister said. And Mother tried to stop him, but he pushed aside her hand and gave the little girl a small sliver of ice. He laughed and they talked quietly, husband and wife. The little boy grew drowsy, curled deeply into his mother and slept.

She took them back down the long wooden steps and out to the sidewalk where the colored lights played. They sat in the warm car, and again the boy drifted into sleep waiting for him to come. But he knew why his mother had taken them there; they had come to get his father.

Something was wrong. She was pacing the living room for hours and saying prayers under her breath. She had a rosary wrapped around the knuckles of her hands and she walked quickly. It was very, very late at night, or very early in the morning, and the boy crawled around the corner of their room, following his sister into the hallway, curious to see what was going on. He had heard his sister get out of bed and had watched her listening at the door. He followed her when she left the room. He sat in the hallway in Howdy Doody pajamas and stared at his mother. She turned and saw them.

"Oh . . . you children. Get back into bed now. *Please* . . ." she said, a curt edge in her voice.

"Where's my daddy?" cried Sister.

"Your daddy's still working . . . he'll be home any minute now." She began to shoo them back to their room. "Don't worry, children, Daddy's okay." She smiled at them, but her lips were trembling.

Then he saw the white armchair pushed in front of the door; the chain was latched and he knew something was wrong. He wanted to ask her why she was afraid, but she was whispering to his sister, calming her. She was tucking him back in bed when the boy heard him at the front door; Mother's head jerked around as if someone invisible had hit her on the chin, and she ran from their room, closing the door. But as soon as she was gone, Sister opened the door and he sat with her on the floor, listening.

The boy could not hear very much, but he sensed his

father wanted to get in the house and she would not let him. She was asking him questions, but the boy could not hear the words, only the voices. Sister was biting her fingers, and when he tried to crawl out into the hallway, she stopped him with her foot. He heard this loud man's voice and a crash that seemed to shake the whole house. And she was running down the hall, into their room, slamming the door. When his father appeared in the hall, he seemed like the biggest man in the world, but he did not look like his father anymore; he was mad, not simply angry, but foreign, wild and glassy-eyed. Father stood there for a moment with the black saxophone case in his hand, his hair tousled like in sleep, his clothes wrinkled and hanging on him like dead skin. He set the case down by the lamp and yelled down the hall. "Nobody locks me outta my own goddamn house! Do you hear me? Nobody!" He shouted it again. He stormed the bedroom door, pounding with both fists. He screamed.

"Daaaaddeeeee . . . Mommeeee . . ." stammered Sister, and the boy started crying with her, terrified.

But Mother would not open the door. He threw his weight against it; he attacked it with his arms, but it did not give way until he kicked it in, once, twice, and the splintering wood pulled away from the door jamb.

Mother was by the nightstand, dialing the telephone. He grabbed her by the shoulders, wheeling her around, wrestling the phone from her hands, and he tore it from the wall so the cord sailed through the air like a snapped clothesline. She screamed, a terrible rippling anguish the boy had never heard before, and his father hit her in the face, again, finally knocking her back onto the bed. He fell on top of her, his knees straddling her stomach, shaking her so violently her hair moved in a brown blur about her head.

"You don't lock me outta my own bedroom!" he shouted.

Her hand lashed out between his legs, punching, grabbing at him until she struck home and his coarse grunt like dull pain filled the room. His face was swollen in a fury not quite complete, rabid, eyes like tiny fires in the darkness, but he stopped fighting and moved backward off the bed.

"Ray . . . Georgia . . . my children . . . my children," she sobbed, seeing them standing in the doorway. ". . . Children, look what he's doing to your mother." Blood stained her face.

And Ray hated him. The boy charged into his leg, biting, tearing, trying to hit his face. But the father only lifted his son into the air with one arm and taking Georgia in the other, he carried them into their room. Ray fought and kicked and cried, and he did nothing to ward off his son's blows; he just looked at him until the boy fell under his own tears. Then Father told them it was all over; he told them not to get out of bed again or he would spank their butts till they bled. "Don't cry kids," he said. "Everything is all right."

3

The interview ran like this; each time it changed in little ways but mostly it ran like this:

Ray . . . mind if I call you Ray?

Sure . . . everybody else does.

Not really true, Ray. I've never heard of a musician with more nicknames than you . . . seems every day I read a new one in the papers.

Yeah, I never understood that shit myself, just one of those things that has always happened to me.

I understand you were thinking of changing your name at one time in the early L.A. days?

It was my first agent's idea. He wanted something that would look better in print, on album covers. Can you believe it? But he didn't last long after that. The name fits the music I play, you know? That razor sound.

So does the face, Ray. There's a real destructive edge to your profile, like frayed light. My bio states that you ran away from home at seventeen . . .

I left home, I didn't run away. It was simply time to go.

An' I seemed to be the only one who understood . . . maybe my dad did.

And it was about this time that you began writing, earnestly working on *Smooth Road?*

That's right. I think *Death Mask* was first . . . then within months the *Smooth Road* album came out . . . after the original stage performance in L.A. A million cheap gigs later . . .

And the movie followed on the heels of the record's success. A remarkable piece of work.

Thank you.

So what do you do now?

Well, after the shows at the Garden, we're goin' to Spain for the winter, do a couple of shows, one in Madrid, but it's not really a tour. I'm going to live there for a while in the sun, buy a new motorcycle, ride around the world . . .

I had my tape player on; it was an old Stones cut called "Live with Me" with a nasty sax bit by Bobby Keys. I didn't hear Lonnie come into the warehouse behind me. I didn't know how long he had been standing there by the door.

"You runnin' *the interview* again, Ray?" he laughed.

I didn't turn around, but his voice shocked me. I looked down at my workgloves, rubbed them together as if I was trying to cover a hole in my palm.

"Where were you?"

"New York. TV show." I picked up a sack of the fertilizer and carried it over to the skid. "Was I talking out loud?"

"Oh yeah. You were riding a motorcycle around the world, bro. I get to go, doan I, Ray the Face?" Lonnie walked over and sat down heavily on the stacks. I said nothing, just kept moving the fifty-pound sacks of horseshit without looking up at his grinning black face. "An' excuse me, but ain't this what they used to call nigger work?"

"Somebody has to do it. You won't."

"Got that right." Lonnie stretched out with his hands behind his head. He was so long, languid, and shiftless, too big and too bold. His body always seemed to be brooding, thin as a rope, disjointed, as if caught in an unguarded yawn. He looked like a bass player was supposed to look, even lying down.

"This fantasy is a trip, isn't it? I mean most stiffs dream 'bout fuckin' centerfolds . . . you wanta be one." Lonnie propped himself up grinning around the empty warehouse. "Vision of yourself, black jacket and boots, red neon sign, smokin' a cold cigarette, maybe a bar door in the background. A photograph they could use on the cover, huh Ray? *Rolling Stone. Billboard.* Your new musical philo-so-phy sweeping panic and chaos through reviewers and agents, through the music bizzness and Hollywood . . . the question they asked on the covers of magazines at every supermarket 'cross the country . . . WHO IS RAY THE FACE?" And Lonnie fell back laughing. "You got a problem with reality, doan you, Ray?" he said, slapping the pile of fertilizer under him.

And I said nothing. It wouldn't do any good to stop him now, just let it run out, like so much ooze.

"Just do me a favor, RayMan, doan ever do Barbara Walters or Merv Griffin . . . you owe me that much."

"One day, Lon, one day . . ."

"I know, I know, you're gonna play New York City to the ground," he interrupted. "Well, how 'bout L.A. tonight? While you been movin' shit for twenty bucks a day, I was busy linin' up a gig for us. Seven at the liquor store, man."

"Lon, not another fucking wedding . . ."

"So, what the fuck is wrong with a wedding?"

*   *   *

Lonnie and a union trumpet player named Pauli walked off the stage in the middle of the set to moon the bride. There was a small recess in the curtain that hid them from the dance-floor audience. Lonnie pushed his cummerbund down to his knees and wiggled out of his tux jacket; he and Pauli linked arms and dropped their pants, bent over, and aimed at the bride, dancing a slow, sentimental number with her father. No one saw it but the band. By eight-thirty we were all drunk.

The groom was shaking hands before the bandstand. Swaying to his favorite song, he'd requested it four times already. "I Left My Heart in San Francisco." He looked like a younger version of his father-in-law, fat, short, baggy-assed, with hairy, plump hands like a gynecologist. He rocked back and forth on his heels, grinning like a faithful dog at his dancing wife of three hours. I looked over at the one black and one white ass pointed at her and turned to find his eyes on me in sudden surprise. But not bothered, simply smiling drunk. He leaned his head to me in confidence, talking into my ear over the music.

"I used to live there," he said, nodding. "Yeah, I used to live there . . . born right there . . . right next to Golden Gate Park." I smiled back. It was pitiful.

The leader turned out to be a dapper old fellow with thirty years of clarinet under his belt, three marriages and no future. As a kid he had played the circuit with Glenn Miller in the swing band days; he even mentioned a few St. Louis clubs that I remembered hearing at home. Names. The Cinderella, the Warwick Hotel. Dad had played there. Now I watched him fronting a put-together dinner band in a Spanish ballroom, enough booze to make him ham it up, waving the clarinet over his head, tapping his patent leather shoe to the beat. His eyes wa-

tered constantly, and I never caught his name. I was lost
for a moment but no one noticed. At the final crescendo I
filled in behind the guitar line, way back, slipping in behind even the trombone. I jumped it a bit to make up,
then the whole set died with an E-flat thud. The dancers
went wild, the bride was curtseying to her father. Lonnie
and Pauli were pulling up their pants. The best man
hopped on stage and stole the microphone. It was time to
open the presents. Break time.

The band hit the bar. The hotel was the Vista Del Mar at
the north end of Santa Monica, nothing but palm trees, a
horizon of ocean, red-jacketed porters and a line of big cars
in the circular drive. The reception was in the Fiesta Room,
the hotel's regionalistic version of a grand ballroom, purely
Spanish with colored crepe paper hanging from the ceiling,
candelabra and miniature pinatas on every table. The waiters were tired old Mexicans dressed as bullfighters. Som-
breros decorated the walls. But a view of the ocean filled
one complete wall, the curtains open to the sun, floor-to-
ceiling purple through the glass. It added what was missing
from the room. A touch of class.

"Ain't you havin' fun?"

Lonnie and the trumpet player saw me staring out at the
water. We all smoked cigarettes and drank quickly, either
straight or just rocks. Every time, every wedding looked
like this. Pauli was a little drunker than he should have
been at this stage of it, cleaning off a silver tray of tiny
sandwiches cut into triangles. Trying to get something in
his stomach. I knew the feeling.

"No. These people terrify me," I said.

Cakes and candles. The Fiesta Room was bulging with
people, black and white, sharp flashes of gold the dominat-
ing color, December-dark tans of the wealthy on the
women, distinguished gray on the men. The flowers were
yellow roses.

"I can't do any more of these, Lon. It spooks the shit outta me."

"Doan look at 'em, that's all," Lonnie continued with a steady humming in his voice. "Poor RayMan. Look 'round, How many brothers you see in here?"

"The piano player."

"That's right. Me an' him. So doan feel too spooky all right? At least you're white. Slap down the free whisky and shut the fuck up, man." Lonnie was laughing to the room as he said this, he was always laughing.

I never knew what it was between us, but it was elementary and inbred in our own puberty: it wasn't particularly fun although there were moments; it was the cold, united routine of our lives, it was shrugs and hugs. It simply went on each day; I woke up in the morning and it was there, like music that was measured by stupid violence and the useless weight of shared hope. Dreams. Dreamers. Lonnie and I never talked about anything. Except music, and that was usually a fight. But here he was right again, with that streamlined blackboy practicality: get drunk, get back up there for another set, get paid, get out. Don't say Thanks at the door.

I caught myself staring at the side of his face. Then there was sudden applause from the dance floor, the room oohed and aahed over a gift of blue china. The father of the bride went into an impromptu speech about friendship. Someone had stuck a piece of cake on the wall by a red sombrero.

"How many mo' sets we got?" slurred Pauli on Lon's shoulder.

I pushed away from the bar, still drawn to the window with the graceful, long breaks of ocean behind it. The bride's purse caught my attention because it was so all alone in the center of the largest round table. It looked like a rhinestone turtle creeping toward the edge; beside it was her white lace veil and the bouquet of bridal flowers. Instinctively I searched the whole room with a quick thief's eye, feeling as if I had already taken the purse, and the thief's plan formed immediately without a second thought. I knew enough about stealing not to think about it, just do it, do it fast. I breezed the table once, no one was watching, their backs were to me on the dance floor, their backs were to me at the bar. I stopped to put out my cigarette at the round table, leaned in over the ashtray and took four envelopes sticking from the open end of the rhinestone purse. I slipped them up the sleeve of my jacket with no problem.

I locked myself in the bathroom stall but did not open the envelopes. I heard feet, and the door hinge open, so I stuck them down my boot, fitted them under my sock. I flushed the toilet.

We began the second set with a lazy, slow-dance number for the old folks. I watched them return to the table, the bride running high with excitement, her cheek stained with lipstick from kissing everybody in the room. They sat and composed themselves with coffee and polite drinking. She didn't miss the envelopes. I could feel the blood rushing to my face, stared down at my fingers working the sax valves unconsciously. I looked at their individual faces, one by one around the table, and my prize scratched against my ankle as I kept time. I felt those four paper envelopes like a ten-pound cast around my foot. Payday. I laughed to myself, clever as hell, making it work for me. The set went by in sweet time.

By ten-thirty we were at the back door to the parking lot and the little leader handed each of us three folded tens on our way out. He spoke quietly with the boys he would use again as if it was some big fucking deal, as if any of these older guys really cared. They filed out in line like so many factory workers with tired cigarettes hanging in their mouths and instruments tucked under their arms, faces like waiters, hands that shook when out of their pockets. The leader said nothing to Lonnie, didn't even look up at me. I would never see him again.

Lonnie was too drunk to be driving, but so was I. He pointed the beat, blue Mustang back toward Venice.

"Let's go to the St. Charles," my voice soft from whisky, "c'mon, Lon." I swung my foot up on the front seat and pulled off the boot. "I wanna spend some of this juice." The envelopes fell from my sock.

"What the fuck?"

"It's my livelihood, Lon," I slapped the paper against his shoulder, "my visible means of support."

"Money in there?" Lonnie puckered his forehead.

"I can feel something." I fingered the first one. "It's either money or free Big Macs." I tore the blue envelope open. Two one-hundred dollar bills. "I stole 'em, Lon."

"Muthafuck you did!" He jerked the car to the curb.

"I took four of these babies out of her purse . . . an' nobody saw me do it!" The second envelope contained two fifties. The third and fourth had a hundred apiece. Five hundred dollars. I made two packs of money on the front seat, straightening them like cards in the weak yellow light. "Which pile do you want?" I asked.

"What're you talkin' about, which do I want?" He bumped the transmission into park and turned to face me.

"I mean we're in this together, Lon." I winked at him over a cigarette stub. "Ain't that the way it is?"

"That's the way it is, RayMan!" He slapped my hand with a loud crack in the night, a smiling bolt of friendship that hit like a rip in the ocean outside. He swiped a pile of money from the seat, stuck it carelessly in his jacket pocket. "That's the way it is." We peeled away from the curb with the radio up loud.

She didn't even miss it. That little purse was jammed full of envelopes like these. I threw the empties out the window.

She had thousands of dollars for her marriage vows, now I had two-fifty for my saxophone. I looked at Lon and he felt good. Felt good about it. Ain't nothing wrong with catching a break, I told myself, stealing's only wrong if you get nailed.

I sat in the dark kitchen, naked on the floor with a package of cookies and a cup of milk. The night was cool, but still I had felt the need to rip myself from these clothes. They lay scattered under the table with the sax case. I glanced over out of habit, just to make sure it was there. It looked like a small black pet, curled, asleep in the clothes pile. Like a little dog that followed me around and gave me something to worry about. The cookie grew too heavy, broke, and I lost it in the milk. "Shit." I cracked open the refrigerator door for a bar of white light to see, and fished the cookie out in pieces with my fingers.

Allie had come into the kitchen behind me, out of the darkness of the bedroom. She knew I didn't see her. She breathed lightly and slipped in thick socks across the cold tile squares in a hushed effort, unsure of whether to disturb me or simply leave me be. She figured I was drunk again. Probably spent all my money, managed enough for a bag of cookies and a carton of milk on the way home. Drank the rest. She watched the hard muscles tighten in my neck, as thin and pale as the moonlight on the window glass. She thought I was handsome, hungry and lean, pushing, pushing, always pushing, handsome like a wolf. Handsome like a man who would have no problem with women, everything else in my life, but not with women. And Allie remembered how badly she had wanted me, wanted a baby with me. It wasn't that long ago.

I stirred to her presence behind me and turned. Allie was naked except for her socks. I smiled and opened the door more to see her in the light. She crossed her feet, crossed her arms over her chest. Her eyes were moody, black hair, blacker eyes, dark strip between her legs that was perfect. She was the most exciting woman I ever knew, I had ever even heard of.

"Ray."

"Shh . . . don't say anything." I got to my feet, pinned her against the sink, so gently placed my mouth on hers that she moaned once in spite of herself. I kissed her hair, so clean. And I was so dirty, smelling of cigarettes and whisky. But I didn't care. I lifted her onto the edge of the counter to enter her standing up, bracing my hands behind her in the sink, crashing the dishes, glasses. Allie tried to speak but I kissed her hard this time and I could feel her now. I was inside of her and I leaned back to look at her, to see her face, her hands on my chest in that swimming light. Her legs were spread and I began to work into her. Then she stopped. Her body just stopped and her mind took over. She didn't push me away, there was no struggle; if I wanted to fuck her I could. But that's what it would be, fucking: don't confuse it with making love. Allie looked straight into me, her eyes slitted as if against a great wind; it meant something to her, she told me that, she told me everything I needed to know without a word. Then she dropped her head. I pulled myself free of her and she slid off the counter.

"It's not working, Ray," she said with dry tears.

"I know."

4

The maid pushes a stolen grocery cart along the hallway. It has been modified to carry her linen, her dirty towels and sheets stuffed in the bottom, the clean locker-room towels in the wire basket. She has the tools of the trade, shoe boxes with Comet and Lysol, scrubs, plastic garbage bags and rags, a spray can of cheap air freshener, and a pair of Playtex gloves with no thumbs. Twine holds the broom and dustmop tied upside down to the back. And like all grocery store carts, it has one frozen wheel, dragging across the worn carpet so that every five feet she must lift the cart away from the wall. Just one more useless thing in her life. It bangs the wall and she swears out, "Goddamnit! Piece of crap!" The sunlight has hit the hallway window, but it is indifferent sun, coming like a yellow plague, showing years of dirt and neglect, warming the locked grate. It is ugly. She is a dark Puerto Rican woman, light moles grown under her eyes like bubbles; she started working this hotel when she was nineteen, twenty-three years of this hallway. And the ones above it. And the ones below it.

The old man slept in 22N. His morning dreams appeared as irregular shapes, indistinct patches of brilliant color, moody expressions of an unclear past breezing through an open back door. Pleasant and restful. His bed seems to have been made around him, the sheet pulled tight, folded across his chest, his arms extend over the pillow, behind his head. Old and very white, he breathes hard through his mouth, the hairs in his nose, long and gummed together in clots, do not whisper in the wind. He hears the maid's cart banging outside in the hallway, he hears her swearing; it stops at the room opposite his door. He tries but cannot open his eyes, the seeping liquid has sealed them closed.

The room's window is beside the bed, and he can see the morning light coming in beside the bed, and he can see the light is still strong, murky, the color of crackers, he thinks, Ritz crackers. The sound of the maid means it is early, before eight, but it is already warm and the room needs air. On the stand is a glass of water and the old man dips his fingers, then rubs his eyes open. He rises slowly from the bed, the residential hotel room is small, untidy, poorly furnished. The dresser drawers won't close, the wooden knobs are gone, and if they close all the way he can't get them open again. The mirror is the face of a medicine cabinet hanging on a black string, the desk and chair are draped over with his clothes. He doesn't pay the extra for the maid service and he doesn't miss it. The window slides up easily since he put Vaseline on the chain and the broken piece of mop handle holds it open. He looks out to the window across the airshaft; an old woman, older than he is, with a dog and a television lives there. He hears her late at night—watching the old reruns with the volume up loud. The dog barks whenever anyone coughs. Her blinds are down. The traffic noise is sounding like thunder when the city trucks pass and everything else melts under them. It is going to be a nice day in New York.

The old man's body is like a lazy white stick; he wears nothing but banded white undershorts, but he has no ass to hold them up, his tits sag like a woman's when he backs to the bed and falls for fifteen more minutes of sleep. His stomach has turned into a belly. It seems to move even when he has stopped. But he has a head of hair fanned out on the bed under him, gray-white and thick and long as the Rasta man's, a heavily lined face and a thin, vexed smile that suggests there might just be one or two more hard-ons left, and eyes that when they open again will be light-blue reckless fantasy.

He is awake now; the old man is leaning on the bathroom sink, he removes the dirty dishes and sets them on the floor. He draws a cup of water without yet looking at himself, drops in a coffee coil for instant Maxwell House. He eats breakfast from a fresh jar of applesauce. He is hungry enough to eat the whole thing, but something tells him to save half like he always does, and let the coffee finish off the rest of his appetite. His movements are very tired this morning.

He has turned on the radio, his building is high enough to pick up the station from New Jersey and the DJ is talking jazz in a low, seedy voice stretching his words like blues notes, the "upcomin' 'traction" and "ladeees night" and other new words the old man cannot understand. But the music is right up his alley; some of the stuff he could remember without trying, remember the color of the album cover, remember buying it, slicing it open with his thumbnail, peeling off the plastic. He had a lot of records at one time. The only thing he cannot remember is what happened to them all.

He shaves with handsoap and a spent razor that pulls and nicks the hang of baggy skin under his chin; he hasn't the stamina for a full shower, thinking, standing under the water is no big deal but the drying-off on a hot morning like this is simply too much work, so the old man washes his face and under his arms, and fingers soapy water through his hair before he ties it back in a ponytail. He can't recall where he put his hat, or even if he wore it the day before.

The old man is dressing. Slowly. Fishing clothes from his beat-up dresser until he finally selects a shortsleeve shirt and a tie, worn yellow summer slacks. And there it is, the straw fedora, on top of the dresser, on top of the ragged, black saxophone case with the cardboard showing like ribs sticking through, and the handle fixed with paper clips. But it seems to be holding.

The morning is still growing outside the window; the bricks now show a sharp angle of sun spearing down to a point in the dark airshaft, but the dressing has tired him and his spirits are weakened suddenly. He will have to rest before going down. He doesn't feel so good, too much coffee, or blood sugar, or some shit like that. He bows his great, handsome head. The room sags in a secret around him. A stranger would see terrible depression and loneliness in this cheap landscape, poverty and the decline of a man like a tattered buffalo hitched to a muddy roadside merry-go-round. But what good would that do? The old man lives here. Says he's lucky to have it.

He yanks his tie a little less tight in the elevator, studies his face in the shiny stainless-steel panel around the floor buttons, and slips a pair of black sunglasses on his nose. He bought them years ago at a gas station somewhere in the East. He thinks he looks pretty good. The elevator is crowded. Other old people who have tried to talk with him in the past and don't try anymore stick to the back, their eyes fixed on the dropping numbers, the green lights. A Spanish mother with three small ones sticking to her dress, and a young girl in a headset humming with music. She is next to him. Her hair is orange and her makeup has been smudged-on in greens and black like jungle camouflage, but her legs are slim and hard, and the old man spends the ride waiting for the doors to open so he can watch her walk away ahead of him.

He moves thoughtfully through the lobby; the carpet is threadbare and he has tripped on it before; it smells like take-out food. It was once a fine hotel, now an SRO, a step away from the street and carrying the stick. The foyer has a marble fireplace and blue furniture already staked out and populated by the blue-veined old who will sit there all day, nap and stare, then struggle back to their rooms for the night. They never make it out of the building. They don't want to.

But the old man carries his saxophone case to the lobby desk and sets it on the counter. A young Arab is sorting mail with his back turned.

"Are there any messages for me?" asks the old man. "22N?"

The Arab does not look up. "Nothing."

"There could be . . ."

"Don't you hear me!" the Arab snarls. "Nothing!"

5

The applause had died away, an echo of a whistle, a shout, murmured deep in my ears; the others had already abandoned the stage leaving just me and Miguel still fucking with his old cymbal stands, tightening down the screws with his hands. The stage was a dangerous piece of work, cheaply built, covered with green carpet, the plywood showing through like tobacco stains under the piano. Green fucking carpet, man. Hard to believe. I stared into the fogged blue spotlights, searching through the tables for the girl. A few lumbered drunks clapped like tactless seals, but I ignored them. She was not there. The chair where I had seen her sitting was empty. I unhooked the horn from the G-string around my neck and set it upright in the stage stand. My T-shirt stuck to my back like plastic, faded dark with sweat under the lights, even the sax seemed to be sweating through its metal skin. I fitted the muzzle over the mouthpiece and stepping back to the amplifiers, used one of Miguel's kitchen towels to wipe off, face, head, neck, all in one motion.

"It's hot as a fuckin' cocksucker in here," breathed Miguel.

My sight passed thick-eyed over the little jammed room

of tables, at the long sidebar, at the dirty, lingering reflections in the mirror. But the girl was not there. Where the fuck did she go?

I had a cigarette at the end of the bar, the flick of the match catching Jello's sharp eye, pulling her smiling to me.

"Ya BabyRay . . . what'll you have?"

"A little Jack an' water, Jello." Still looking for the girl, I didn't notice Jello had dressed for the night, tight skirt and sweater. Heels, and barefoot as she worked the bar! She clicked her teeth at me as if she were pinching sexy bites of my skin.

"I doan understand anybody that drinks Jack an' water with crushed ice." She sat the Collins glass before me.

"Makes it like a slush, you know."

"Okay." She mopped the counter, white towel in her black, work-weathered hand; she was thinking up something to say to me. "You really steamin' it out tonight. Too bad there ain't nobody here." She said it like a joke.

"Tell me about it. This is Latin shit-music."

"You're doin' it all right. You all right with it, Ray the Face." She ignored a fat man waving an empty glass, and leaned over the bar on her elbows at me. "Baby, what're you wearin' later tonight? Anything on? Little breakfast maybe?"

"Breakfast," I laughed. "Me an' you, Jello?" I laughed again, shaking off a cold timidity, laughing through a shiver. And she pulled away, retreated. "But you didn't happen to see where that chick sittin' at the top table went?"

"Didn't notice." She cut me off, blowing smoke at me.

"That black chick with the really pretty face."

"Ah said *Ah didn't notice.*"

Jello turned suddenly, left me standing there alone before I could tell her it was just a joke, a bad joke. I threw my arm out in disgust, and when it came back it struck something hanging there on the chair. A leather purse. Dangling waist-high, the chair was empty, no one was looking. Before I had thought to take it, the woman's wallet was in my hand. So quickly it didn't feel like stealing. It felt like this: the weak glare of bar lights hung blind in my eyes, an uncanny moment, standing quite still now, nothing alarming at all in it, but a rhythm of confidence in my easy breathing, a surging of streetkid purpose. I was acutely aware of a thick glass of red stir-sticks at my elbow, of the fruit tray of cut limes, lemons, twists, and olives. I opened the catch, fingered the tube roll of money, the sharp edges of new bills. My free hand lifted the cigarette to my mouth. The smoke was hot. Jello was giving me the freeze, no one was looking at me. I felt suddenly very sleepy. Tight-muscled in the hinges of my jaws, the first impulse of nerves, the first real impulse to steal the money. The bar got longer, as I looked down it, running away from me like a stretch of steaming asphalt. And I couldn't do it.

I closed the wallet, called out to Jello while flipping it casually on the bar. "Hello . . . hey, Jello, somebody dropped this on the floor."

She came, opened it. "Money's still here," she whistled. "Lucky. Somebody's a lucky somebody."

"Yeah. Good." I took my drink and disappeared down the dirty back hallway. It was lined with empty Bud cases stacked halfway to the ceiling, kegs standing in sticky puddles of their own stale beer. Garbage-stuffed cans by the alley door. It stunk. The ceiling dripped fat umbrella beads of moisture over a single yellow lightbulb in the EXIT sign.

Outside it was cold. The sky spilled a milky haze like light dust over the blackness, four or five stars, but their shine was no match for the streetlights' low bluish light. I pulled off the T-shirt and draped it over the bars on the back window, hanging it upside down so that it might dry before the next set. In the cold air steam rose like thin lines of smoke from my naked chest; I wiped dry and left the towel on my shoulders.

"BabyRay . . . o'er here." Lonnie was in the shadows down the alley leaning his back into the brick wall. I could see the white in his eyes, the red glow of the joint he smoked.

"Here man," he said handing it to me.

"Is it straight?"

"Yeah, it's a sissy stick." He grinned. Lonnie knew that I didn't like to smoke any shit, heroin or cocaine, but every now and then he'd give me a spiked one just to watch my face turn. He was reading a newspaper in the dark and looked up over it at me. "Sound real bad tonight, Ray the Face, almost like you mean it," he said.

"Not exactly sweet city music, is it?"

"Damn, man! Only a goddamn fool idi't be standin' out here with his shirt off. It's fuckin' cold, man . . . makes my balls shrink just to look at you." Lonnie pushed away from the wall and nodded to his newspaper; when he grinned it was as if his teeth were stacked against the bricks.

"Check this shit out," he started. "This cat made up thirty thousand fake car phone antennas . . . you know, ain't no phone in the car, just that little fake antenna on the back like he's got one. Sold 'em for twelve ninety-five. Sold all of 'em, Ray . . . thirty fuckin' thousand of 'em."

"That's L.A., man."

"That's L.A." He was quiet for a while then, and I was tranced off staring at a black spot of alley, but I could feel his eyes on me, I could feel Lonnie getting ready to say something. He was about to give me some shit.

"You missed a couple of the fatman's cues again."

"Fuck him," I answered.

"Right . . . fuck 'im. It's only a gig. If I'd known you were so *busy*, man . . ."

"Lon, he plays everything as straight as six o'clock."

"He's the one who's payin'."

"An' I blew Manny out on purpose. All he's doin' is the desperate fatman trot . . . Latin shit-music." I bitched.

"Put your shirt on, man. Look, he's a wired-out loser, lookin' for somethin' he doan even know what is."

"But he's payin'," I cut him off.

" 'xactly."

I slipped back into my shirt too stoned and pissed to say anything more, thought running away from me. I thought I could hear the ocean breaking, but it was only Lonnie crunching ice in the back of his mouth.

"RayBird, did you see that little girl sittin' out there?"

"Yeah, where the fuck did she go?"

"Man, she had a smile like she'd already killed a dozen men." He laughed harder, slapped his big hands together.

"Christ, Lon, she was starin' right at me. I couldn't . . ."

"Starin' at you!" His eyebrows arched high. "Man, you be dreamin' again. That girl was lookin' at me." And he held up a flat hand like punctuation. I shook my head. "Man, you're a sucker for any black chick that smiles at you. Face up, I mean you're my friend an' all, but you just a skinny white kid. You ain't *even* pretty." His laughter carried a hint of disguise. "Now. Look o'er here at me. My steady drive bass . . ." and he danced down from the waist. "She was lookin' at me. This little girl is a whole basketful of shit-blues trouble . . . better leave this girl to me."

"It's never hard to find you two jerk-offs. I just follow my nose down the closest alley." There was a new voice crackling in the alley, Manny stood behind it. "Blowin' dope down som' cold alley, huh?" He shrugged sloping, middle-aged shoulders; his words had a clever bite. "You guys dig the image that much? Hard jazz hoodlums? Aaaaagh . . ." and he pulled mucus up his throat like clotted syrup and spat it on the ground.

"Makes me laugh," he continued. "I used to be like you hard cocks, young players with nothin' to lose, right? Feed that hard, cool image, dope, booze, women . . . an' wit' more fire than you got. Until I became a real player, a leader. I don't need it, man." And Manny stepped out into the night as if he owned it.

Lonnie gave me the big eye, crushed out the roach, and slipped past Manny back inside.

The older man turned in the quiet light, his face profiled in the shadows but now visible, the lines stretched across his forehead showed strain. Dead brown eyes, age-betraying hands fluttered at his neck.

"And you can dig this," pointing his cigarette at me, "you can play, you know it, and I know it, but I'm runnin' this show. This is my quintet."

And sensing the drift, "Look, Manny, I'm sorry. I blew a cue. I was feelin' good."

"Hey, man, I'm talking to you." He paused briefly. "I sat on the piano bench for years, years. I'm a Spic, a Mex, Greaseball, huh? I played more bullshit than you can remember hearin'. Years! I hated it. But I played 'cause I wasn't the fuckin' leader. Now I am. We play what I want, and how I want it played."

"But Christ, Manny," I tried to slip by him.

"There are ten thousand cats like you, man, just waitin' for a chance, so if you want the work, when I cue you out, you get out. You follow me. Got it?"

I said nothing. Manny walked back into the club.

The club was almost empty for the last set. I checked the line of faces along the bar, quick criminal smiles, hard characters, brothers with sinister eyes, sharp-lined jaws. They came to score—drugs, women, any fast midnight buck. How many came to hear Manny's Latin All-Stars? The regulars with lead in their veins, drunk on Jello's watered booze like they were every night, these mouths of

twisted teeth jawing at each other through the smoke.
"Fuck this," I said softly to myself, but all I could do was
watch them.

And brooding within the silence and innocence and igno-
rance of myself, with a strange pinpoint light in my eyes,
I saw the black girl again. I knew I had to look at her, that
it was only a matter of seconds until I did. She had her back
to me, her small shoulders erect and unmoving. I watched
her absolutely black hair, the magic animation as her earrings caught the light. Watched her long fingers press
against the tabletop. She looked clean, exciting. But she
was not alone. Lonnie sat grinning across the table, grinning at her. And there were two sharply dressed black men,
one with a gentle old face and white patchwork in his hair,
vaguely familiar in his mood. And the other a hustler up to
his hatband. He spoke with hands, showing off his rings.
That kind.

I shook the moisture out of the sax, fingering the key-
work, fitted a new reed, clipped it around my neck; I was
the first up, going through the motions blindly, like a mechanic, all without looking at the girl. Then Lonnie was
next to me smiling behind his stand-up bass, a smile so
fucking big it almost sizzled. "You know who that is?" he
whispered in my ear, didn't wait for an answer, ". . . that's
the King, that's fuckin' who."

"Coleman King?"

Lonnie nodded. "Makin' a comeback from the grave."

Behind the bar Jello clicked on the house P.A. "Ladies
and Gentlemen," she announced in monotone. "The St.
Charles Club brings you more live jazz. Now, Manny Mon-
toura and his Latin All-Stars." Manny strutted an entrance
from the side, looked like a Mexican gas-pain, sat down at
the piano and tickled a quick, right-handed riff. The last set
began.

And who really gave a fuck about these moments? About

this music? I didn't. I didn't know why anybody was there except Jello and the drunks. And the jukebox. I kept from looking at her. And when the time came for my solo I took it slow, pulling away in a long, building swell, pinching my eyes closed. Playing loud. Spread-legged. Fevered.

"Sexual . . . that's the way the horn should be," the King said to the girl, but she barely heard him.

I strained groaning streaks of notes at the finish, then layed out as Manny cut in his own lazy piano. I opened my eyes; she was looking right at me, waiting. I half-turned, aware that the table was watching me, swore to myself, goddamn, goddamn. I was angry and cool; Lonnie was smiling at her too, he was thinking about her too. And in that momentary flicker she was aware that we were friends, placed together side by side on the same stage and it hit her with a cocky irony that made her smile like a women who has sensed it all. Everything.

"Ladies an' Gents . . ." Manny suddenly waved the band down and cut in on the piano mike, ". . . Ladies an' Gents, please, please . . . Anyone in this room who knows anything about jazz at all, will by now realize that we have a living legend here in our audience tonight. What more can I say? Ladies an' Gentlemen . . . The King!!"

The man at the girl's table stood, and the house went wild with applause. He smiled, nodded.

"C'mon, people, maybe we can persuade him up here." Manny yelled in the mike. "Coleman, come up . . . Coleman King." Manny motioned him onto the stage. And the King had his horn case right there with him.

Manny waved me off. I caught Lonnie's face in a sideways glance, but no one noticed me leave the stand. No one but the girl. She applauded the King and her eyes followed me. I slumped down at an empty table offstage, lit a cigarette, wiped my face with my shirt.

Coleman King was cool; he shook Manny's hand and

nodded to the boys. He carried his horn in competent hands that took no notice of it. Center stage. A photographer materialized and began popping flashes. And the King was a pro; he stepped up into the good light for him, hammed it. Manny kicked off the piano blues riff.

I watched from the back. The little sharpie at the girl's table had orchestrated the whole scene. The suit had set the whole thing up for King. He leaned back now, whispered something funny to the girl. Waved good-bye to the photographer.

The girl looked until she found me.

What kind of game is she playin' anyway? I turned away. Pissed at myself for being made a fool, and I was swept with a queer feeling that I was ruining my whole life in this one set, that I would never be a player.

It was a bad time to sell the bike, a bad day, cloudy as mustard and cold. I had a cigarette going, looking at the sky and the bike on the sidewalk, the kid crawling over it as if he knew what he was looking at. I would ask for more money if I could wait until spring when the weather turned warm again, and the boys in jackets got careless and itchy for long stretches of oceanside road. I was always like that. One of them. Selling a motorcycle in the middle of winter was fucking stupid.

"Looks like the can needs gaskets all over."

"Probably right."

"Let's try kickin' it again," the kid said.

We pushed it down the street for another block and a half but she wouldn't start. Couldn't turn it over.

"Hasn't been fired up for a while, huh," the kid laughed at me. He knew he had a good deal now; what could I say to his price?

"She runs like a bitch, man . . . just too cold." And goddamnit, I didn't want to lose my bike. I sat back on a garbage can and couldn't even touch it now. The ol' BSA was gone, the Beezer was gone, I knew by the cold delight in the kid's eyes. It was about the only thing I'd ever owned, the bike and the horn. Hey, Look I Don't Think I Want To Do This . . . I said the line over and over in my head, waiting for the right moment to say it to him, and then I started remembering too. Allie had loved the bike in the beginning. I would pick her up downtown after work in her dress and high heels, and she'd climb on the back in front of all her lawyer buddies, and we'd roar off making them shake their fucking heads. She loved that part, making them wonder who she really was. We'd fly down PCH to the beach and sit there for hours watching the sun, then ride slowly home. But remembering was just begging for it, asking to get slapped in the face again. The kid was holding out cash in his hand, "I don't know what to say, Ray . . . she won't even start, you know."

I left the money on the table with the bills where Allie would find it when she came home. I had another old jazz gig in Redondo Beach and I started to walk. I had plenty of time. I kept looking up for that burned clay sun in the sky but it never showed. It didn't take long to come to a block riddled with little children playing through the sidewalk litter. They had cut fingers and bruises and trembling, Spanish smiles. Two dogs chased sticks up the street, their hair was greased and spiked into knives over their backbones. Laundry hung embarrassed from the windows, trying to dry on the wind like cigarette breaths. The little ones, the babies, sat on the curbs and mouthed handfuls of dirt, the windows were open inches at the bottom, and I could hear the voices of their mothers and smell milk burning in a pan.

Three boys stopped me at the end of that long sulking block, hands out. They tucked their chins back and stared at me with keen, childish intelligence, and mucus welled in the corners of their eyes. "No dinero, man," I said walking through them, "no dinero." And I thought it was strange that I found myself thinking of Allie, in her office, with people floating in and out with important papers and lunches and phone calls, business deals and half-serious flirtations. She probably had her shoes off under the desk. And I was walking through the ghetto feeling like a saint. It was just strange.

I watched him count the money.

Bobby Turner was the slowest man I'd ever met. The great Bobby Turner, the man they used to call Soul on Rye, two-hundred and forty pounds of melancholy leaned back in a card chair, rubbing a stubby finger along his chin, then up his pink tongue for a hit of spit, and back to straightening the bills. So they were all faceup, all pointing in the same direction. "Way the bank teller likes 'em." He said the same thing every time he counted money.

He sipped from the mouth of a long-neck Bud, a trumpet-playing man for thirty-odd years, a style of jazz mellow in the extreme. Jazz for lovers. It was a quarter to three in the morning and I was tired. The back room was hissing with steam heat and armpit sweat and the stink of Bobby's jasper cologne.

"Hey Trump," he called out, "you got two tens for a twenty?"

Trump came in from the hallway and handed him the tens; he held a hot towel to the back of his neck. Trump had arthritis high up in his spine and the weather was killing him. He looked a hundred and ninety years old, his eyes twenty pounds of yellow apiece when he turned them on me. He had been with Bobby since they were kids in Georgia; he said things like, ". . . playin' the rounds wit' Bobby Turner'd put ruts in Dick Clark. Wear 'im out." He played piano with his face three inches from the keys; his neck was always sore.

"There you go RayBird." Bobby held the money straight out. He wasn't getting up for me.

"Thirty?"

" 'at's wat we said, isn't it? Thirty bucks."

"Yeah." I tucked the money into my pocket. "So that's it . . . you don't need another night?"

"Naw." Bobby grinned at me. "Don't be sweatin' it, man. You got good routines, you still young."

Trump was still standing there, waiting for his twenty.

"I just can't get a steady gig." I stopped at the doorway, "I need work Bobby, I'm broke."

"You should be playin' rock 'n' roll . . . that's where the money is . . . 'cause you got the talent, f' sure, man, you got it." Bobby pointed his beer bottle at me. "You knew it was a sub, didn't you . . . jest a fill-in."

"Yeah." I nodded. "Thanks Bobby."

"You still young . . ." Bobby said, ". . . that's the trip."

"Yeah." I picked up my sax case. "See you Trump."

Trump didn't say a word.

Three A.M. Cold city rain blown by the wind between the buildings, and this bar was a beer-an'-shot joint buried alongside construction for the new hotel, the next shopping plaza. And stepping out the back door, I saw the freeway loops first and the rain second. The sky was so low I could see clouds moving in the shallow asphalt puddles. I should have felt better than I did about Bobby's compliment, I mean the guy had been around for a long time, played with heavy people. But it just didn't mean much.

*   *   *

I fumbled my way across the darkened room following the rectangle of outlined yellow light in the window shade as I had done hundreds of nights before. The seams of light met on the bed and I sat down. Allie remained stiff and silent, careful that an arm or a foot did not intrude into the cold center of the bed. I inched toward her but stopped short of touching. I wouldn't cross the line either. I was still thinking about walking home in the streetnight that I loved, about an atmosphere that breathed and swelled as I did. It was music racing by. No moon sky. Rain. The low buzzing of overhead power lines, a crackle I never heard in the daytime, only at night when it's so loud. I was thinking about music and money, money and music. About a shapeless Sears store with a burnt-out neon S, so it read EARS in the black, about a bum in his doorway, a red scabbed face huddling in an old Navy coat, about his lips working as he slept like a suckling baby, hugging a dead bottle. Money. Music.

"Sleeping?" I whispered. Allie did not answer. "I saw the weirdest thing tonight, on the way home . . ." I continued to talk to her, very low, ". . . a cat had this pigeon down by the wings . . . right on the sidewalk before me . . . held it there. And I didn't know that pigeons could scream like that. I spooked the cat and the pigeon got away. But it was weird as hell." I sat next her her, didn't really know what to do. I didn't feel like getting into bed like this. But there seemed to be nothing else left of the night. She didn't hear me, but I said it. "I loved you baby. I was never bullshittin', Allie." And I really believed that.

6

He opened the black case and lifted out the powerful gold saxophone. With a small cloth he polished the big horn, fingering the pearl buttons, opening and closing the flat valves. He wiped away the moisture and the finger prints, buffed the large, circular mouth. He removed the silver mouthpiece protector and fitted a new reed. He blew through the horn, running up and down the notes, up and down his fingers moved from button to button, then he stopped and adjusted the reed until it was right. When he blew through the horn his cheek puffed out as though it would burst, and the blue veins in his neck swelled thick, knotted. His face seemed held in pain, and his son, watching, wondered how he could hold his breath that long.

"Come over here, BusterBoy," he said.

"Look, now, I'll hold it for you and work the valves. You just put your lips around it like this . . ." he made his mouth half open, ". . . an' squeeze the mouthpiece when you blow through it. Okay? You got that?"

"Sure, Dad."

"Okay, Try it." Ray blew as hard as he could into the horn. It made a long, harsh sound, a squawking shutter. The old man laughed.

"You don't have to blow that hard, BusterBoy . . . just try it like you're blowing up a balloon. And don't pout your lips like that. Grip the reed with your lips . . . *Gently*. Okay. Try'er one more time . . . go ahead."

"James, don't make him play that . . . that god-awful horn if he doesn't want to . . . I should think that one saxophone player in this family would be enough," his mother's voice called out from the kitchen.

Father wet his lips as if he were about to answer, but did not; his face held a look of failure now. Lean failure. He wiped the spit out of the mouthpiece and ran up and down the notes very fast and very loud. Up and down, up and down, screaming music. His fingers seemed to move on their own impulse without him directing them. Then he stopped.

"That's called runnin' the scales." He grinned and had a cigarette.

He got up and went to the old portable record player. He had bought it a long time ago. He put on a record, turned up the volume and sat down to play along with the music. Now the saxophone no longer screamed; the notes flowed out smoothly and with chilling feeling. He held a sound until his face turned red, then moved on with the music, the saxophone laughing as he played. When he played like this the boy's skin crept up in gooseflesh. He played and Ray turned to the music, touching it, feeling it on his face, seeing it before him. His glowing saxophone matched the woman's voice perfectly, the words, the notes were the same.

> You made me leave my happy home
> You took my love an' now you're gone
> Love brings such misery and pain
> I guess I'll never be the same

Since I fell for you
  I get the blues 'most every night
Since I fell for you . . .

At six o'clock he dressed in his sport coat and black tie
and taking the black case in one hand, he kissed Mother
good-bye and left the house. Ray watched him until the car
pulled away down the street. And when he was gone, a
great quietness filled the house.

7

I had heard the story about Coltrane, that he used to practice in the bathroom facing the wall. I liked that. Gave me a picture of him alone. The great man alone. The bathroom was cold, but I didn't mind, I liked it petrified cool, old-tile cool, textured porcelain and green rusted metal. And the sound was good. I stripped to a T-shirt and jeans, barefoot and easy, playing the sheet music from an Ornette Coleman songbook, the pages ripped out and spread on the floor. I played it upbeat and as nasty as it would take and still be the same notes. I wanted to play jazz like rock 'n' roll, and I knew it could be done. I sat on the toilet and played with my socks stuffed in the bell to keep a lid on the noise. It was Saturday and Allie was home; I think she was home, I hadn't been out in hours. When my back stiffened, I moved around the tiny bathroom, watching myself in the mirror, standing in the tub, blowing with my eyes closed. I liked looking at myself as I played this way.

Just play, just play, I told myself, you got nothing else to do. Just play until the walls run with sweat. I hadn't worked in weeks, a long dry spell with no money. And Lonnie was a pain in the ass; he didn't want to practice, he didn't want to do anything except talk about Reggie.

She was a singer, she was this, she was that, they were putting together a band. And he was borrowing money all over town just to keep taking her out. But I wasn't any better, taking money from Allie's purse for cigarettes, waiting until she got home from work so we could eat. And we hadn't made any real love in so long, fucked a few times because that's what animals do when they sniff each other, but when it was all over and she wiped the spot off the sheets with her dainty little ball of tissue, there wasn't a lot to say. Thanks. What's for dinner? There was always too much to get out from under anymore, so I locked the bathroom door and the ashtray mounted with butts and roaches smoked down to the stain . . . just play, just play that cold thing in your lap. The rest of it doesn't exist.

Outside: "Ain't that some shit." Lonnie listened at the bathroom door, grinned, poked his thumb at it through the air. "He's playin' in there," he whispered to Allie who stood next to him nodding her head. "It's that same damn song . . ."

"All the time. The same thing." Allie didn't like Lonnie and she always watched him through a half-squint, squeezing her face down from the eyebrows. But she'd let him in. "The latest kick . . . sitting on the toilet, playing that fucking saxophone. All day," she complained. "I have to knock on the door and ask to use it."

"Ain't that some shit," Lonnie said to himself. And Allie stepped away from him. He knocked and I opened the door.

He was dressed in black, shaved clean, ready to go out. "Look at you, man," he said with his hands outstretched. "RayBaby you're a fuckin' mess. Look at you!" His eyes went to the sheet music, to the ashtray, to the clothes, to me.

"You look like shit on a stick, man." Lonnie looked about

the floor as if he could not look at me. "You writin' any of this down?" he asked.

"You heard it?"

"Yeah. I heard it."

"I don't have to write it down."

"That's cool." Lonnie pulled the socks from the horn with two fingers. "These clean?" And I nodded. "Well put 'em on, man."

"Why? What's the thing?"

Lonnie closed the door, came into the bathroom with me. "The thing is money. We gotta get some, we gotta get some tonight. I wanta run some shit an' I need you."

I looked up at him, trying to find his eyes. "You're talkin' crime . . ."

"Yeah, I talkin' street crime, man, plain an' simple."

I shook my head.

"What're you supposed to do, Ray? Sit on the toilet and starve? I need money. You need money . . . she ain't gonna give you anymo'," he pointed at the door. "C'mon, man . . . it was your idea, RayMan, the wedding, stealin', keepin' us alive to play music . . . was it all just talk, Ray, big fuckin' talk?"

"It's different, Lon . . . all you want is to spend it on the little girl." I stood quickly, startled him, grabbed his shirt. "Look at me, man, when you talk to me, look at me. If we're gonna get into this shit, you better be able to look me in the eyes."

"I spend it on what-fuckin'-ever I want to, Ray the Face."

"Then find somebody else." I let go of him. "An' don't worry about me."

He stammered about, lit a nervous cigarette. "You doan get it, RayBird, Reggie can do big things for us, both of us. She knows people, man, music-biz people, people we need to meet. People we need to get the tapes to. If this band of hers comes off, we got people behind us. Dealin' her is just as much *music* as sittin' alone in a fuckin' bathroom dreamin' about it."

"Find another guy. Not me."

"Then dream in one hand, white boy, an' jack off in the other. That's all you got," he yelled and slammed the door.

Lonnie told me the act was clean. All I had to do was walk up to the vic and ask him for a match, Lonnie would take him off from behind. Quick. Out of there. He told me he'd done it before, when he was a kid. We sat in his car in a Studio City parking lot; I looked over at his face in the darkness and saw hesitation, heard the sound of lying in his voice.

"Right, Lon."

"What's that mean? I did it before, Ray . . ."

"Right, Lon. When?"

"Oh, man, you know I did spend a little time out there before I met you. It was all part of the trip." Lonnie fell back into the seat, slapped the steering wheel. "Man, Ray . . . You're so fulla' shit sometimes."

I laughed. Lon was half-turned toward me with an attitude on his face, slipping into a bit of his street nigger thing, the same way an actor changes dialects. Lon was just a guy I knew, a friend, but he was a black guy and he had that over me and at times he *had to use it.* Funny, he was always out of character as a street nigger.

"Okay . . . okay, so you're tough an' cool . . . the only thing is, the only thing that makes sense is to let me do the action," I said.

"What? Again wit' that . . ."

"We're gonna hit a white guy. I walk up to him and he'll remember everything about my face—blue eyes, long blond hair, ponytail, leather jacket, you get it, Lon?" I gave him a moment, then continued. "You're black . . . in the dark, if you keep your chin down, wear the tam, come up fast on him . . ."

"I'll be just another nigger," he interrupted, sat back to think it over. I nodded.

"Can you do it, the action?" he asked.

I got out of the car.

We picked a short guy in an open, tan trenchcoat. He was alone, coming across the parking lot at a quick pace, in a hurry, one hand fumbling in his pocket. Lonnie stopped him cold, in front of him so abruptly Lon never had time to ask for the match. The guy backed up right into me. I grabbed him by the coat behind his neck. "Don't hurt me, please . . . please." He began to cry almost at the first grip. I was surprised; I pushed his head forward. "Please, just don't hurt me." A cigarette dropped to the ground by my foot. I hadn't even seen him smoking.

"Don't fucking turn around, asshole," I yelled at him. Too loud.

"Cool man . . . chill," Lonnie said holding his palms down. He was watching the parking lot. The action was mine. I planted my fist in the middle of his back like a warning.

"I don't want to hurt you. Give me your money," I said almost in his ear.

"In this pocket . . . this one." He slightly raised his right arm. I clutched him tighter at the collar, put my hand in, came out with a fold of money. I took his wallet, then walked him to the nearest car. I pushed him face down on the hood, said "Thanks, man."

We drove around splitting up the money, a hundred and twenty bucks each. "I couldn't believe he was crying. I hardly touched him," I said for the third time.

"He was a fuckin' faggot." Lonnie wrote off the whole crime. "The guy was a faggot . . . he almost fell over."

"He was scared all right." And I was thinking to myself, Why? I wasn't going to hurt him.

"Let's get another one." Lonnie turned up the radio.

I had Lonnie drop me at the liquor store, told him that I wanted to talk to Keeber about something. He was going on to see Reggie, meeting her at a restaurant in Hollywood. Reggie and the little suit-and-tie hustler from the St. Charles Club. His name was Cody Orleans; Lonnie fished his card out and handed it to me, NEW ORLEANS, INC., MANAGEMENT, CODY ORLEANS, PRESIDENT.

"You know how much it costs to print up ten thousand of these?"

"You see, Ray the Face, that's your problem . . ."

"About fifty bucks." I cut him off. "Lon, I don't want to hear bout it, man. Just drop me at the store."

He left me at the curb, under the big red neon MIDNIGHT LIQUORS. Lonnie could not understand me, my mood, my anger. He called me "pissy mothafucker," and we let the whole thing drop. I watched him make a right turn and disappear. We had mugged two people and pulled it off. I had two hundred dollars in my pocket; unconsciously I rubbed my hand over it. He had called the last victim Pork, and that stuck in my head, Lonnie'd said, "Shut up, *Pork.*" I had never heard him use the word before. It was done and I didn't feel bad about it because I didn't feel responsible. Already the night had taken on an image of abstract reality, scenes I had seen or heard in a bar somewhere. No different than playground fights as a kid, more memories, and I found myself wondering if Lon really had done it before, the action? In any case, now we had both done it before.

Across the street there was a crowd at the 7-Eleven, police cars, two paramedic wagons; the cherry-top lights were spinning without sirens and two cops were walking off the area with yellow tape, pushing back the sidewalk traffic. The scene of a crime.

Lights were on in the rooms over the liquor store; Keeber was up there with some buddies playing cards. It was a corner building, square brick-face, old Venice. I passed through the double glass doors setting off the barking buzz of the electric eye, and a young black man jumped up from behind the counter.

"Jesus, Ray . . . it's jest you," said Tyler.

"Yeah, Tyler, just me. What'samatta with you?" I moved passed the racks of skin magazines to the counter. "You're almost white."

"I got the toughest job in California," he said. Behind the counter he had a *Penthouse* open on the stool and a short, black-taped baseball bat in his hand.

"What the fuck is wrong?" I said again, nodding at the bat.

"I'm spooked an' Keeber doan give a fuck." Tyler was maybe twenty-two, a plain, wide-faced black from Inglewood trying to work for a living and do the right thing for his wife. He wasn't very bright and everyone from his parents till now had ignored his good heart. "They took off the 7-Eleven," he said, pointing across the street, "killed the counterman . . . some girl too."

"Jesus."

"Jesus, right." Tyler came around and led me back to the front window. "That poor brother was younger'n me, Ray . . . shot his ass right off the floor. You shouldn't heard it, man." Tyler ducked down, juked his head from side to side, "I went right down on the floor . . . it sounded like fuckin' Beirut or some shit like that. You oughta go look at it."

"I don't want to go look at it."

"An' all Keeber gives me is that goddamn stick. What the fuck good is that?"

I shook my head slowly in sympathy, but in my mind I was hearing this high voice from a tan trenchcoat: "Don't hurt me, *please* . . . just don't hurt me."

"He's got a piece upstairs, but he won't give it to me," Tyler was saying with his hands resting in his pockets.

"Get yourself shot, Tyler."

"Jest to keep it under the desk." He pointed back at the counter. "That's four take-offs this month. We're the only store open between here an' Monica." He paused when I didn't say anything, then said, "You oughta go look at it."

"I don't want to see it."

"There's still blood on the floor . . . I mean blood, man, not jest lit'le spots. An' bullet holes everywhere . . . took out the glass doors, killed a girl who was buyin' milk . . . you believe that shit, Ray? Jest buyin' milk."

"Is he playin' upstairs?" I turned away from the window. Walked Tyler back to the counter.

"Yeah. Three other guys. Ten Speed's one." Tyler looked at me as if that should make a difference.

"Give me a pint of JD, okay, Tyler." I dropped two twenties on the counter, ". . . an' break that up for me."

I was quiet going up the stairwell behind the beer cooler; nearing the top I could hear the men's voices, smell the stale air. "Daddy's pullin' a wheel," somebody laughed. Then, "Daddy ain't pullin' nothin' but his snotty pud . . ." and that was followed by Keeber's deep, raspy laugh, his great voice commanding and indecent.

The door to my old room was open; I stood under the transom unnoticed through the thick smoke and the breathless heat of the bid. The brown paper shades were down on the street-front windows, the cops' red flasher blinking through dull as my own heartbeat, red blink, red blink, red blink, red blink. Men hunched over the table, above it a cord, a bulb, a roughly cut circle of cardboard for a shade. There was a body asleep on the couch, a yellow light reflecting like the inside of a bag in the bathroom. It had looked better when I lived here, but not much. And I remembered the first night I brought Allie up here, so drunk she threw up twice and slept in her clothes.

"Goddamnit . . . sonofabitch." The hand went down, Keeber raked in the pot surrounding it with his giant paws.

"Now, now, don't get nasty wit' ol' Keeber . . . only 'cause you in a raffle you can't win . . . uh uh uh uh," he laughed, holding a cigarette in his teeth. He poked his head up suddenly at me in the doorway, "Well, lookie 'ere, lookie 'ere. It's the Great White Horn. C'mon in, Ray."

"Hey, Keeber, how is the ol' man?" I said.

"I don't know, where is that *ol' man?*"

Ten Speed nodded at me. He pushed his chair back from the table and stretched his arms out over his head. He was a wicked, sharp-faced kid, rigid as a police photo; he was young with white teeth and deep, thick-looking skin, like hide. He thought he was all right.

"Hey, Ray the Face," he said grinning, "you here to play?"

"Yeah, how you been?" I asked, but didn't wait for an answer. "You got a chair, Keeber? What's the game?"

"Low Ball . . . fifty an' a dollar," said Keeber, pulling out the folding chair beside him. "Where's Lon?"

"Hollywood, with this Reggie girl." I put my whiskey on the table and Keeber took the first sip.

"That boy, Jesus, that boy," Keeber slapped his hands together. "Girls gonna kill 'im. I know it . . . he'll do anything to get a pull up their dress. *Anything.* You giggin' tonight?" Keeper asked as I put my money on the table.

"Yeah, yeah. Silly restaurant thing . . . a new restaurant, you know . . . background music," I lied badly.

"Where?"

"Marina Del Rey." I was trying to say anywhere but the Marina. I looked up as the cops' flasher suddenly stopped on the front shades.

"About time," said Ten Speed. "You hear about it?" he asked me.

I nodded. I turned to Keeber, but he spoke first.

"Better him than me," he said. "Where's your horn, Ray-Man?"

He was dealing the cards now, very nonchalantly, very cool, not looking at anything but the table. The other player was a cab driver named Fisher who said nothing.

"Shit!" I faked it, again badly. "Christ! I must've left it in the car."

Keeber stopped the deal and looked at me. It was like he was stepping on me with his eyes. He put out his cigarette and then we played cards.

In under an hour I had lost all the money I put on the table and I pretended not to have more. I had already made a mistake with wise ol' Keeber. He knew that I was lying about the night. But it wasn't the first time he'd been lied to by Lon or me, and that was another way to look at it. The game broke as I left the table, and Fisher tried to wake up the man on the couch.

Keeber said to me from behind, "Where's your head, man? It sure wasn't in cards."

"Keeber, could I get my old room back, you know . . . if I needed it?" I said a little too softly. "I could pay rent."

He took a long time to answer. "Where would I hold my game?" His grin was so sly I didn't know if he was kidding or not. Then he went very straight. "If it gets tight." His look was eloquent, it explained everything in an instant. He knew Allie and liked her, but never mentioned her name, as if she was out of this negotiation.

"I wouldn't ask unless it was already tight."

"What's Lon say about it?"

"Okay with him."

"Then don't worry 'bout it." Keeber placed a hand fatherly on my shoulder. "Doan worry 'bout it, Ray." He stepped to the table and his cigarette pack. "It's not like you to be travellin' without your horn," he said.

"Yeah. Not like me at all, is it?"

But Ten Speed caught me at the stairs; he was waiting on the first landing. On his way out, he said. I could see the hustle working in his mind.

"What kinda' high you got goin', Ray the Face?"

"Bunk weed. One of your buddies sold me, why?"

"Better, man," smiled Ten Speed. "Look." He held out two reds in his hand. "Man, these the real thing, too. Three grains, get you stoned. Not bad price."

"Jesus, Ten Speed, I don't want any fuckin' reds. How much?"

"Half a buck. Good deal. If you can move some quantity I can do you thirty-three apiece, but it's got to be in the hundreds."

"You think I'm movin' caps for you?" My sneer cut him back. "Remember last time I played with you?"

"RayMan, c'mon. Hey . . ."

"I got my ass burned. No, you wait!" I stared into his shit eyes, dry-swallowed what felt like a toothpick caught in my throat. "What the fuck do you think I am, Ten Speed?"

"C'mon, not true, not true, man. I didn't know . . . I got fried worse'n you. I didn't know. I thought we had that all straightened out." He held out his hands like a TV preacher. "These are pharmaceutical, straight from the hospital. I got the whole jar."

"Good. Have fun. I'm not a drug dealer."

"Since when?" he grinned at me.

"Fuck you." I turned.

"Man, musicians need bread too. Here, take these." He slipped the pills into my pocket. "See, Ray the Face, that's

the beauty; you're a night owl, you're always around people, fellow musicians, you know, other night owls, people
who like their drugs."

"I'm not movin' drugs for you, I don't need money that
bad." I was free of him, heading down the stairs, thinking
about the fresh, night air, how good it would feel on my
face. I didn't turn around to see Ten Speed flip me off
behind my back.

8

He could see the clock behind her head, 4:00.

"Ray, Ray, Ray," she paced before him with a pointer in her hand. "Have you been practicing at all?"

"An hour a day, Sister." The other kids giggled.

"Your diatonic scales need much more work. I expect a marked improvement by the end of the week, or I'll be seeing you on Saturdays."

"Yeah, Sister, all right," he said closing his music book.

She turned and glared down at him, perched for an instant on her toes, but she eased back and said nothing. She would let that one pass.

He closed the door and dropped his geography book, and the saxophone case banged into his knee. Kenny Thomas picked up the book and handed it to him. As they walked across the concrete square, he looked back to see her shutting the top windows with a long pole. They locked eyes.

"What'd you do Ray? God . . ." asked Kenny.

"Nothin'! I didn't do nothin'. Damn nuns are just goofy, that's all. She's pickin' on me 'cause of my dad."

"Naw. They don't do that," Kenny shook his head. "Nuns can't do that."

Ray stopped by the square-cut hedge that separated the

parking lot from the football field. He knew he was gonna get his ass kicked as soon as he saw them. He felt it first in his stomach, then running like current in his legs. There were five of them flipping a football around, flattop haircuts, dirty necks, and in the middle two boys, older boys, Butchie DeFalco and Pauli Frayis. They loved to fuck with Ray. He saw Butchie wink. Ray wanted to run; if he was alone he'd run like hell. But Kenny was there beside him with the same foul stink in his guts, and he couldn't run. He didn't want Kenny to see him run. So the two boys just walked on, short, quick, dirt-kicking steps and pretended that everything was all right when they should have been beating it the hell out of there.

Pauli threw the football and Butchie ran after it, but as it went over his head he lowered his shoulder and smashed into Ray. Kenny was knocked to the ground.

"Why don't you queers get the fuck out of the way," Butchie said, squeezing the ball in his hands.

Ray stood there. They had circled around them in seconds. He looked at Kenny, but did not help him up. Butchie held the football to his lips, like a fat trumpet.

"How was pansy practice? Huh, bandsy, pansy." They all laughed.

"Why don't you leave us alone," said Ray, looking around for any kind of help. "We're just walkin'."

"How long's it been since you had a pink belly, Ray, Ray, Ray? A nice pink belly," and Butchie was almost funny, the way he pushed out his mouth, the way he blinked his eyes like a caged owl.

Behind Ray they were repeating it, "Pink belly . . . pink belly." And Kenny's eyes were terrified, and Ray was looking at him and thinking, Don't Cry, Goddamnit. Don't Cry. Tennis shoes shuffled around him. "Wanna pink belly?" They were closing in, waiting for Butchie to strike. "Wanna pink belly," and Ray asked himself, the nuts or the head? If he missed . . .

The nuts. "Fuck you!" The boy howled and swung the saxophone case up hard, catching Butchie inside the thigh, and he screamed. Pauli sucker punched him in the neck from the side and Ray went down. He couldn't see anything. On his back in the dirt, choking, the dirt in his face, their hands grabbing his arms and legs, holding him down. His mouth was coated white with spit. He got punched in the face and started to cry, couldn't see anything but arms and heads over him, arms and heads with no sky in the gaps. No air to breathe.

They tore open his shirt and since a good pink belly needs for the skin to be wet, they spit on his stomach until they had a little puddle, and Butchie began with a hard flat hand, slapping, wap . . . wap . . . wap . . . then faster wapwapwapwapwapwap. And it hurt. Ray cried out squirming under them.

"Stop! Stop that! You boys!" The nun was coming across the school yard waving her arm. They punched him once in the stomach and ran.

"Fuck you! Fuck you, assholes!" Ray yelled after them, throwing handfuls of gravel at their backs. And trying so hard not to cry, he couldn't stop, but not because of the pink belly or the punches, but because he could never pay them back. Never in a million years. Kenny sat in the dirt crying.

"Shit Kenny! Jesus."

"Fuck you!" he flipped the finger at them.

"Ray, Ray . . . are you hurt?" The Sister brushed dirt from his back and fussed at his hair.

The boy wiped his nose with the back of his hand, smudging the dirt with watery snot on his cheek and looked down at the red patch of his belly, still pulsing with blood so close to the surface it hurt. He picked up his sax case. The Sister laid her hand on his shoulder, a hand like a cold, steel claw. But Ray shook it off, looked her in the face. "Fuck you too," he said. And ran.

He walked down to the river, staying close to the railroad tracks and following them home, just glad, finally to be alone. They have moved again, the third time in two years, this time into a house owned by a relative; it was a wood slat house in a part of town that was going black. It was farther away from school, but the boy didn't mind the walking; it was cool this time of year, with the catfish-smelling breeze kicking up off the Mississippi and black-birds soaring into the sky. A gray sky moving each day into winter. Ray understood why they moved so much, around the same town without really going anywhere, like crickets in the same crackerbox, corner to corner. It was because of money.

Ray understood more than his parents thought. He listened when they fought, often sitting against a wall in the next room, or under an open window on the porch. He heard his father call the relative Cowpie, because he was a farmer and smelled like cow shit. And Ray knew, although his mother would never say it, if their rent was a little late, Cowpie would have a hard time throwing out a relative. Ray listened when they fought:

"He's family, James," his mother had said.

"*Your family,* not mine," his father had answered. "Tell him to shove his factory job down some other poor bas-tard's throat."

"Please . . . they're only trying to help us," she was almost begging him.

"Help us? What's wrong with living here by ourselves for a change? We don't need your damn relatives." He was pacing by now, smoking cigarettes. "And how am I supposed to play, Elaine? Have you thought of that? Huh? How in the hell am I supposed to keep my chair in the band and work night shift at the plant?"

"And how are we supposed to live? James, you have a family, two children in school. Your responsibility is to them, not to that second-rate band."

"Second-rate band! Second-rate . . . Goddamnit Elaine!"

"You know it is!" she was shouting back. "They don't pay you anything . . . you drink away what you get in one night. My nurse's salary is not enough to raise a family on. We need money!"

"It means I play one week out of every three . . . this job . . . it means I lose my chair." His voice was quieter now, choked by her strength, by the truth. "Goddamnit, is that what you want?"

He went down and signed up the next day. Cowpie made good on his promise to Ray's mother and got dad a job. It was the worst job in the mill, at the lowest pay scale, a scraping two dollars and thirty cents an hour; they called it "workin' the pits," down the metal ladder to the half-block-long, three-man-wide concrete ditch that ran under the steam rollers of the fabricated paper machines. The temperature in the pits was usually ninety to ninety-five, and in the St. Louis summers it could go as high as a hundred fifteen degrees. He was the only white man on the crew, but he told his son he liked it better that way. "Cuts a lot of bullshit," he said. Their job was to drag out the steaming, wet-paper waste that ran from the rollers above into the pits as the machine trimmed the cut, and feed the waste back into the pulp vats. The air around the pulp vats was sharp, like gasoline and puke mixed together; in the pits it was worse because the steam baked the smell right into your skin.

Ray had overhead Mom's relatives talking, saying, "He

won't stick it out. He won't last." Some even said that Harold had arranged the pit job on purpose. But he fooled them. He worked hard, missed a few days when drinking heavily, but not many, and he turned his money over to Mother, for the family. And he kept playing with a terrible, hungry pride; every weekend and whatever nights he didn't have to work graveyard or swing, he filled the first saxophone chair in that second-rate band. They played whatever dance hall or club spot they could get. He saved this money for himself, "reed money" he called it, and kept it loose in his pocket. He played and drank and stayed out late and the family couldn't touch him as long as he worked in the pits.

Ray could see the mill in the distance now; two white-brick stacks whirling strings of wind-blown black smoke. The plant sat on a flat-rock landing where the railroad tracks and the Mississippi came together. His father was in there, feeding the vats, stoking those white stacks.

Ray walked on, throwing rocks, breaking the old green-and-brown booze bottles as he found them, just to hear them pop, and thinking confused picture-thoughts of his father sweating in the pits with the niggers and his mother in her white nurse's uniform waiting in the hospital. He didn't know why he thought of them so much like that, and it seemed weird to him, like something was wrong, like he wasn't normal. But at times Ray couldn't get them out of his mind.

He heard a train coming. He crossed the tracks to be on the clear side, set his books and saxophone case down. He searched his pockets for a penny and, in luck, came up with two. He placed one, with Lincoln's head facing up, on each rail and waited there, the big, yellowed glass eye shining, the backward-funneling tornado mane of coal smoke, the cow-catcher grin, a damned awful whine of screeching metal noises that sucked at his shirttails and hair and pulled the high weeds around him like crowds of cheering friends. Ray waved and pulled his arm up and down at the elbow until the conductor let go two quick blasts from the steam whistle. She rumbled by, swaying to each side, like an old woman, eighteen dumper cars, no boxcars at all, carrying loads of coal and sulphur and limerock, and stuff like that, to the factory. An old man, striped overalls and cap, waved a red hanky from the caboose and she was gone. Ray jumped to the rails and peeled off his two pennies; they were big as a quarter and thin as a page, Lincoln's head stretched way out of proportion, like a face through a fishbowl.

The boy ran along the chain-link fence to the gate and said "Howdy" to the funny old guard sitting on the stool in his glass booth by the turnstile. He wore thick eyeglasses placed low on his simple nose, and a brown uniform with a string tie and a gold horseshoe around his neck; his belt buckle was a silver plate that spelled out "Texas" and he had a goddamn big pistol holstered on his hip. But he was a friendly old guy, not really a cop at all, and he let Ray wait for his father inside the gate. "They ain't come out yet, but I 'pect 'em any minute now," the guard said.

A long file of men came walking across the graveled lot; almost at the end of the line, Ray saw his father. He ran to meet him, and his dad saw him coming fast and started to laugh. He lifted his son, rubbed his head.

"Waitin' for the ol' man at the gate are ya'," he smiled. "Well, I'll be damned." He turned to the man walking beside him. "I'm a lucky man, though, ain't I. This is my boy." And the man agreed that he was one lucky man.

"BusterBoy," James said, noticing Ray's tattered shirt, "what the hell happened to you?"

"Mom's gonna kill me . . . it wasn't my fault, Dad. I swear."

"Fighting?" And Ray nodded. "Who was it?" asked his dad, now bending down to look at him closely.

"Honest, Dad, we didn't do nothin'. Kenny and me were just goin' across the playground, you know, after practice, and Butchie DeFalco and his gang, you know, tough guys, eighth-graders, jumped us and tried to give me a pink belly."

He placed his hand under Ray's chin, rolling his head from side to side, checking out the scratches on his neck. "What happened? Are you all right? Hurt anywhere?" And he opened his mouth and felt for loose teeth.

"Naw, I'm okay. I got in a couple of good shots on Butchie, though. I got Sunday-punched and they almost had me."

"Your hands okay?" He squeezed Ray's fingers one at a time.

"Yeah, Dad, I'm okay, honest, but you got to tell Mom that I couldn't help it, these guys just ganged up on me."

"Where's your horn?"

"Oh, yeah, I left my stuff over at the gate." And Ray saw what he was driving at. "The horn's okay too, Pop."

He ruffled the boy's hair and let his hand fall to his shoulder and they walked again. "Good. You look like you came through it all right. And don't worry too much about Mom. Now go grab your gear and come with me over to the Credit Union and we'll take care of some business.

And it made Ray feel important just to be with him.

Ray heard him arguing about his paycheck and watched the woman grudgingly hand him money over the counter. "C'mon, Ray," he said, and they pushed through the greasy glass door. He took his son to the company canteen and bought him a Snickers bar, and a pack of Camels for himself. A pretty young waitress smiled at James. "That your boy, Jimmy?" she asked.

"Yeah, this is my BusterBoy . . . good-lookin' kid, huh?"

"Sure. Takes after his dad . . . he's got your eyes."

Ray blushed red and turned away from them; the big sign over his head was black metal letters:

OWENS-ILLINOIS PAPER AND BOX CO.
A Division of Owens-Illinois Glass Inc.
Plant No. 7, Alton, Ill.

After that it seemed darker than it should have been: Outside the sun was low, shining purple and red through the thunderheads, all else was deep gray, so dark that Ray almost bumped into them as they turned the corner. If it hadn't been for his dad's hand, he would have stumbled right into their game.

They had a piece of plywood up against the fence, a backstop, around which five of them squatted on their knees, so close that their shoulders rubbed and jostled each other as they jumped about, their heads bobbing up and down, white teeth laughing or cussing in the same breath; they were all niggers and under the brims of their hats Ray could see nothing, only eyes and silhouettes. "Jeesus mutha' shakin' shoes, shakin' shoes, gwine down." "EIGHT! Ah be yo' daddy." "Fo' bits the 'ard way." Their huddle was so tight that Ray could not see the dice on the ground, only hear the rattle as they hit the plywood and catch glimpses of the green money that shuffled at their feet. "Shakin' achin' eightin'." "Dou'le fo's, dou'le fo's." "Busted seven, sen' this nigger ta heben." Two other men leaned into the fence above the game, watching, their fingers hung loosely through the chain-link like black hooks, their faces lit by the glow of cigarettes that slanted from their chins. One of them spoke.

"Hey, Jim-m-m, wat's gwine on? Shake some bones?" He flicked his free hand at the game.

"Naw," James said, shaking his head.

"Come on, Jim-m-m, dat louseee pits' money ain't wort nottin' anyway. Might's well drop it 'ight 'ere." They both laughed.

"Naw, Mitchell, not tonight. I got to be gettin' my boy on home," and Dad dropped his hand on his shoulder.

"Yourn boy, huh?"

"Yeah, Mitchell, this's my son, Ray. Ray, Mitchell's one of the men I work with. Say hi."

Ray held out his hand. For an instant, Mitchell looked a little confused, even bothered, but then he grinned a giant's smile and pulled his hand free from the fence. His hand was large and calloused-tough. Like a leather baseball glove, it swallowed the boy's white palm.

"Well, Ah am pleased ta meet ya, young Ray," he laughed, and the other man on the fence laughed too.

"Is 'his a horn case yo' got 'ere?" he asked, pointing. Then, "Does 'e blow the horn too, Jim-m-m?"

"Yeah, Mitchell, he's gonna be better'n me."

"Well, goddamn."

"Jeesus mutha' fuckin' Christ, my homeboy nigger!" one of the kneeling men yelled, and grabbed his cap and threw it on the ground.

"Let's us move over 'ere," said Mitchell, and he gripped James's elbow and walked them away from the dice game. "Now, what Ah wants to know is, is yo' blowin' 'round somewheres tonight?" And he offered a drink from a bottle he carried in his back pocket.

Dad took a swig and fished a cigarette, and Mitchell lit it with a flip of his lighter; in the light Ray could see his face was big, round and fleshy, the color of tree bark, eyes half-closed under his sloping forehead.

"Yeah, Mitchell, thanks, yeah we're playin' a spot tonight, Friday and Saturday at a joint called the Cinderella Slipper Club on Main in East Woodriver. After that, I don't know; they're talkin' about a spot in St. Louis, but I don't know. I jump to goddamn graveyard next week anyway."

Mitchell nodded his head as if he would remember. They talked and had another drink from the black's bottle. But the boy was watching the headlights go down the river road, thinking his own private thoughts and he didn't hear them. Soon his dad said good-bye to Mitchell and he nudged Ray to do the same.

And Mitchell laughed and slapped his leg, saying, " 'ye, young Ray."

As they walked away, Ray turned to look at him again, but it was too black and the boy couldn't find him. The factory lights shone across the dirt road, throwing headless shadows, disappearing into the river, leaving only the lights, flickering like long strips atop the muddy water. A rowboat's oars slapped, stringing a line for night catfish. Catfish! To Ray the whole world smelled like catfish. Without thinking too much about it, he laughed a little and said, "Boy, Dad, that Mitchell's a black ol' nigger, ain't he though, goofy."

"Buster, I thought I'd taught you better. I thought you knew better'n that."

"What, Dad, what?"

"Callin' people niggers like that, what's that?"

"But they call themselves niggers all the time, didn't you hear . . ."

"Can't you see the difference? I mean, really think about it, Ray." He pushed his hair back from his forehead. "Son, you're a musician. *It's all color.* You can't even think words like nigger an' be any good."

Ray nodded his head, he was too ashamed to look at him. And he was afraid of him too. In the electric light his face had a queer bloodless color, a light that stabbed in his eyes.

"Not for people like me an' you, son, not us." James finished and they started to walk again. He lit a Camel and looked out over Ray's head at the Mississippi drifting by. "Don't take it too hard . . . C'mon."

9

There were two of them. Later on, still frightened, sucking his cigarettes down, ashes settling on his shirt's belly, the store owner would tell the police there were definitely two of them. Black. Young guys. Flashlights puckered on and off over the gravel, moving like a family of ducks in circles; other black and white units were already leaving, cops' arms hanging out the windows blue and careless.

Did he see their faces?

No, no, they kept him pushed into the car, sorta like a half nelson, his face flat against the roof.

So, he didn't see their faces?

No, but they talked like niggers talk, they were black all right, they called each other nigger nicknames.

What were they? The nicknames?

Bird and Slick.

Slick?

Yeah, pretty sure it was Slick. He was the bigger one. The little man remembered without hesitation. The two took him from behind in the parking lot just as he reached his car. See? He still had the keys in his hand. He owned the store for over six years, just built in the addition last summer and put the games in there, Pac-Man and Star Command, because he was getting the kids' business now, the old people were moving out. Inland. The beach was getting too rowdy. But he'd never been robbed before. They broke the glass in the door one night, but the alarm went off.

OK. So they pushed him into the car roof. Then what? It was too dark, he knew that; when he turned off the lights in the back it got pretty dark. That was his fault. He knew that. He didn't see them at all, one had him by the hair forcing his head forward, while the other caught his wrists and wrenched them behind his back, *Shut Up Pork, Shut Up.* He was helpless. He had the bank deposit bag tucked into his pants under his belt, let his shirt hang out to cover it.

Did they seem to know he was carrying it?

They found it pretty fuckin' fast. That's all he could say.

Did he see the weapon?

No. But he felt it, right here, that little dip in the back of his neck.

A handgun?

Yeah, it was a handgun all right, felt like a fuckin' cannon. They kept callin' him Pork, they pushed him into the front seat of his car and said they wouldn't kill him. And that was it. They left the car door open. There wasn't much money in cash, thank God, a ton of checks, two hundred and seventy-three in cash. He wanted to know his chances of getting his money back.

Not good.

I stood before the window of the music store before going inside. The instruments were poised like mannequins shooting glints of wicked sun, and I liked to look at them. They were things of life, a band without players. A thousand years from now a case in a museum. A clerk, long-haired, bird-necked, they called School because he was so young, saw me from the back of the shop and started laughing. He always laughed at me, and I never knew why. I guess he thought I was hopeless, a sad case, and that was funny. School took the soprano saxophone from the stand case behind the counter and brought it to me.

"You look like you're reelin', man," School said for no apparent reason.

"Not that bad," I said. I accepted the horn, held it lightly, squeezed the mouthpiece gently between my fingers. "I got some more." We moved to the cash register and School picked up the money I placed on the glass. He took a black notebook from the register and entered the payment.

"How much is it, Ray the Face?" he asked, as if it was too much trouble to count it.

"Ninety-three bucks," I said grinning. "How much is left?"

"Still meaty. Two thirty-three . . . half the devil."

"Let me see that." I read the book, my column of entries. Two hundred and thirty-three dollars to go.

"It's a big toy," chuckled School.

"Yeah. School, can I take it in the back?"

"No problem, Face, no prob." And School scratched his arm. "I wish to fuck I could let you walk with it," he shrugged.

"That's cool." I knew the way to the back storeroom so School left me. I closed the door behind me. By the ramp was a big tin trucking door that bounced the sound off fairly well. I faced it with the soprano. I was determined: By the time I owned it, I'd know how to play it.

"How did you get my number?" I had never talked with her before, but I heard her voice and knew who it was. I started to pace the room carrying the phone.

"Lonnie."

"Put him on."

"He's not here, Ray." She had a blues voice, a little cigarette rasp in it that made her sound older, bigger than the tiny body and delicate features. "He said he was on the way. You know Lonnie." She laughed, then there was a silence. "You should come, it's gonna be a session."

"You're taping it?" I asked, not caring, just searching for something to say, something that didn't sound stupid. Questions musicians would ask each other.

"Yes." Pause. "Hold on . . ." Abruptly a man's voice cracked on the line, the tone was stiff, businesslike; I instinctively knew this one too. "This is Cody Orleans," he said quickly. "It's my invitation. You're hard to find. I've been callin', did your girlfriend tell you?"

"No." Pause. "You remember me?"

"Yeah. You're the groove player. Lonnie says they call you Ray the Face." He chuckled. "I like that, that sells. But here's the thing . . . we're gettin' some people over here an' playin' some music. I'm in the business of finding new players, Ray the Face, an' you're a new player, slightly used from the looks of you." He liked laughing at his own jokes. "Lonnie says you're good, Reggie likes you. If you can't make it, well that's another story . . . but you don't want to miss this."

"You playin' rock 'n' roll?"

"Whatever Reggie wants," he said seriously. "Here she is . . . talk to her."

"You guys jam in a studio?" I said sarcastically. "You just get together and fuck around in a studio, try a few things, tape it . . . that's not too bad."

"Friend of Cody's. We get to use it. Why not? Lonnie said you were a pain, a purist, a sufferer. Well shit, Ray the Face," she scolded me lightly, "get your white ass on over 'ere. We don't believe in sufferin'. We believe in bustin' it open." And she hung up.

When I got there Reggie was singing the blues, old John Lee Hooker. The studio was a small one on the ground floor of a building on Fairfax, all the way in the back, Studio Bee it was called. I heard her before I opened the inner door, ". . . serves you right to suffer . . . serves you right to be alone . . ." She was dressed all in black, sitting on a stool behind a screen with a deep mike; she looked like a photo off an album jacket. She sang with her head tilted to one side, reading the music from sheets on a stand; a young black kid played a lone guitar in a chair across the room. The kid wore a Yankee baseball cap backwards and played the guitar as easily as most people hum. What a look, I said to myself, feeling the door close behind me, the look was perfect. Reggie, the kid, the studio lights, and Cody Orleans behind the glass in the mixing booth smoking a cigarette, just like a producer. Along the wall in the dark sat Coleman King with his saxophone across his knees, a floppy hat was pulled down over his eyes like he was sleeping. I didn't know what to do. I felt frightened by the professionalism; I mean everything looked *real.* And I was so sure it was all jive, I was so so sure they were hustlers living a dream, talking about it, just talking like everybody else. Like me. But Coleman King was there. And the kid was good. And Reggie's voice was practiced and raspy and filled with heart. She sang without moving.

Cody Orleans looked up and shaded his eyes and saw me at the door. He grinned and motioned for me to sit against the wall; he tapped a finger over his lips. I nodded and tiptoed to a chair beside the King. The room was still, and I was aware of the tenseness tightening, tightening in my arms, like rods around my chest. My hands felt too heavy for my wrists, cold, without blood. I was trapped. I couldn't leave now, and the fear came up like fucking vomit. Could I play with these people? Was I good enough? I had walked in here so sure I knew the score. I had them all pegged and fitted into slots under me. I was safe in my bathroom, I was safe playing alone in my dreams and I had pegged them like I had pegged myself. My father. But it was to late to walk outta here, I had to play. I could not leave now; I wouldn't make the door without falling. I put the case down and sat on my hands to stop the shaking.

Reggie finished, the kid played the line out to a fade. Cody tapped the glass with his ring.

"That was fun," Reggie said.

And beside me Coleman stirred enough to raise his head. "She thinks ol' John Lee is *fun,*" he scoffed lightly, running a pair of tired eyes over me. "Fun . . ." he shook his head and then was quiet again, slumping back with his head resting on the wall.

"I'm Ray," I said in a voice that escaped from my mouth. "I'm . . ."

"I know who you are."

He lifted two fingers in the air between us. "My pleasure."

Cody was talking to Reggie by the booth with his arm loosely hanging over her shoulder, and once again I was struck more than anything else with how perfect the picture seemed to be, like a pose. Coleman was quiet but fidgeting in his chair as if he couldn't quite get comfortable and I couldn't take the silence.

"Excuse me," I said to him, "but what are *you* doing here?"

He looked at me out from under the hat and coughed out a laugh or two. "Nuttin' else to do, what's yo' excuse?"

"I mean, you don't need to sit 'round like this and jam." I fumbled it badly. "What I'm trying' to say is, this is just playin', you know, practice. You don't need this." And I felt stupid when he didn't bother to answer. "Or is somethin' else going on here?"

"Naw," Coleman yawned, "Cody's 'ust buildin' the girl. You know, the classic star-maker shit."

Coleman King came forward, straightened his chair on the floor, shook the hat off his head and caught it in his hand. I never realized how large his hands were until he wiped them over his face like stiff brown towels. His shoulder bag was on the floor, a black leather bag covered with backstage passes. He opened it and pulled out a beer.

"I'm gettin' old," he said sheepishly, "can't sleep anywhere but bed anymo'." He slapped the card chair. "I used to be able to sleep in a chair like 'his one fo' hours at a time." He drank and held the can out at me. "An' what the fuck're you so nervous about? Want a beer?"

"Sure. Naw." I lit a cigarette. "Naw . . . I don't feel nervous, it looks kinda big-time, that's all. I didn't know what to expect. Want a smoke?"

"Quit." He laughed, rubbed his finger across his teeth like he was brushing them with beer. "That's 'ust Cody's way . . . the big-time look of things." And the old man focused on me, on my face, as if suddenly remembering. "I saw you," he said. "You can play."

I heard him, but paid no attention, Reggie was coming across the room at me, smiling. She pushed her hair back over one ear. "Couldn't stay away?" she said.

"Nothin' else to do," I said.

And it was very subtle. The way intimidation turned to excitement. I didn't notice the change until I was playing in a chair next to the King. The playing was no great shakes; he didn't look at me while I was constantly watching him, every move, every frown, every twitch of his fingers on the keys. I didn't have much to do, keep the rhythm while Cody had given all the embellishment to Coleman and Reggie with her voice, the kid Dancer with his guitar. It seemed for the most part I was just observing, as if Cody Orleans was bringing me slowly into the circle, slowly so that I wouldn't notice that I was being brought in, and slowly so that the players wouldn't get bent. But the excitement was physical and very selfish; it was for me, like a second set of nerves added to my body, like a slit in my stomach with the magic poured in. I was there, in that room! It was me! The light in the middle of the studio was strong white ovals, overlapping bright, locked-in so that shadows were black as deep space. Outside the light I couldn't see the walls; we could have been anywhere. The air was light, rolling with waves of sound, brittle with music. This was excitement, and sitting there at a break I tried to describe it to myself and found it personal and selfish, like a drug shot straight through a soft spot in my head, in the brain, in the blood.

"Here's a thing, Ray the Face," started Cody, standing before me with his shirtsleeves rolled and a cigarette. Man, he could act. He walked around giving suggestions, making it happen, that was his thing. Bossman. "Here's a thing . . . that's nice . . . what you're doing there is real nice, but it should be a waaa-baaaab-baaa-baaa-waannnaaann kind of thing, shouldn't it?"

"Sure." I set down another of Coleman's beers; he must've had a case in that black bag.

"Follow Reggie's voice through it," Cody winked. "But that is a real nice *color* you get. Don't lose that color."

"What the fuck's he talkin' about?" I asked her when he was back in his booth. "What the fuck language is this baaa-waaan-baaaab-waaan . . ."

"It's the Orleans tongue, mon." She spoke to me in reggae. "The island shit, mon . . . very Ireeee in Hollywoods, mon . . . the language of the coo-coo."

She was standing beside me now, and I could smell her. Her breath was cool as she circled behind me, around the chair, letting her hand touch my shoulder but so lightly that I couldn't be sure. I might have imagined it. I glanced over at Coleman. He too followed her about the room when she moved, he too smelled her in the air about us. Reggie's eyes climbed to the ceiling, then fell on me, very round, holding a faint challenge, and there was a moment of expectation while I watched her lips, thinking that something was coming for me, something was waiting there for me.

"Coo-coo," she said.

I laughed and dropped my beer. There was a noise from the dark and Lonnie flew into the room; the shadows were hanging on his back and his face stood for a shattering second in the light. He was high. The room changed again.

"Man, I'm sorry Cody," he apologized to the glass booth. "Man, I am sorry. Been playin' long?"

"It's cool, Lon," Cody spoke into the mike.

"Nothin' big," said Reggie as he turned to her. "Runnin' some blues with these fellows." She pointed at me.

"Yeah, baby." Lonnie held her and lifted her off the floor. He kissed her and she didn't fight it. But she didn't encourage more. Reggie squeezed his hand as if to say this is not the place, then returned to her screen and headset.

"RayMan." Now Lon turned to me. His eyes were gold. I got up as he came to me. He hugged me, whispered. "Did a solo. Action. Pork action," he grinned.

"What are you, crazy?"

"It was a piece of cake." He bent and opened up the bass case. It was a new Fender, a jet-black beautiful instrument that I had never seen before. I looked at Lonnie but he wasn't paying any attention to me, now. I sat back down. I looked at Reggie, but she had her head down to the music sheets. Lonnie talked to Cody in a calmer, familiar voice. As if they were old friends. Cody seemed to accept it. "Just give me a second, Cody," Lon said. He took a wrapped box, a present, from his jacket pocket and placed it gently on Reggie's music stand. "This is for you, baby," he said, and went back to his guitar.

Reggie was surprised and fumbled to say something, then bit off the words and simply shook her head; but she smiled wide and her eyes glistened in the spotlight. She was happy. She pulled the ribbon gingerly, opened the present in her lap.

I was remembering this:

Going home. I ran down the chain-link fence again, in my longest stride, feeling the warm flow through my body. And it was getting on to serene sunset again, animated beauty above the river, steel-gray and rose complexion. And thick-eyed Tex leaned out of his glass guard booth and told me I was too late.

"Sorry, son, you 'ust missed 'em. Your dad's already come through . . . couldn't've been more than ten minutes or so."

Well, I could still catch the ol' man before he got home, I thought, and started running along the dirt road by the river, and as I did, the factory's outside spotlights flared on and I was caught in their spreading beams, dazzled for only a few heartbeats, a faint ripple, before I could go on. I saw him. He walked out from an alley, the first street after the factory, at the end of the dirt road; he was over a block away but I knew it had to be Dad, the way the arms and legs hung loose, the shoulders well back, head up, the slight dip as he walked. I was sure. I started to yell at him, but before I could he got into a black car parked at the end of the dirt road. I ran to the car, the sax case banging against my leg, and pressed my face against the window.

"Hey Dad, what . . ." A black woman sat behind the wheel, her eyes wide and white, a small gift box, half-opened, the ribbon torn from the top, the wrapping paper ripped around the edges, in her lap, her hands held the little white box. He had his arm around her shoulders and pulled it away when he heard my voice. He looked at me, too nervous, oblique heartstabs of sight. I guess I'd never seen him look like that before. I ran away.

The session got smoking but Cody didn't like it much. I saw the moment in the booth when he stopped taping and that's when it got hot. Coleman King brought a nickel harp out of his bag and played the chrome off of it, played the living fuck out of it, and Lonnie and the kid Dancer stood up and followed each other off. Reggie started singing "Tobacco Road" but it turned into "House of the Rising Sun" and then into a scat cover of "Let It Bleed." She was fine. She was worth whatever it took to get her. She wore Lonnie's gift of a long silver necklace. It had a few pearls in it too. Cody sat in the corner chair and pretended to be digging the jam, but I knew he wasn't happy. He wasn't calling the shots. Coleman King's harp was calling the shots and there was no way to shut it off. The man was old and tired, but he was a genius; the music just came out of him; he was a magic pit, he was an ice cube melting in the sun. I played very well. At one point I looked at Cody with a sudden realization of why the King was there; Cody brought him to make us play better, all of us, Reggie his star in particular, maybe, but all of us played better with Coleman in the room, in the chair beside you. Cody was very smart. I wouldn't ask him any questions after that.

"That's good. That's good with the harp," Cody said, applauding as he walked over. "That's enough with the harp. I mean it's fun, Coleman, an' you play the holes outta it, but we're not gettin' anywhere. I think what we were tryin' to do . . ."

But the King suddenly stood and tossed the harp back in his bag. He started packing up the sax. " 'at's okay wit' me," he said. "I'm tired. I'm goin' on home now." He looked at Cody. "Do what you want."

Cody drew him away from the rest of us. "Coleman, you're not upset?"

"Nooo, Cody, noooo. You don't need me here. I'll just go on home to the bed."

"Okay, man . . . it is late." And Cody went back to Reggie. Lonnie stayed close to her, nodded his head at whatever Cody said to her. I asked the King if he had another beer left.

"You don't need to take this shit," I said to him in a low voice.

He laughed in my face. "Don't be excited, Ray. None of this is for you either, man." King pointed at Reggie. "I know what he's doin'. It's okay wit' me . . . I signed the papers. Cody's hookin' up the new blood to the ol' blood . . . it's nothin' but the two-way transfusion, baby." He threw his bag over his shoulder with a weary heave. "You're just 'ere for the ride." He grinned at me and left without saying good-bye or any of that shit.

And I thought he liked me. I was puzzled, staring at the door long after the old black man was gone, thinking: That's the way it is, nothing personal, not music, not business even, just the way it is. His ability had brought him fame, but that was gone. His ability brought him the freedom to play until he was tired enough to go to bed . . . to sleep.

Lonnie broke my dreams with a hand on my elbow. His eyes were warm; he was a good friend and his face was easy enough to understand, sweet and blank like this, he wanted something. Lonnie almost always touched me when he wanted something as if he needed the contact to make it sincere. "RayBird . . . I was tellin' them 'bout your songs, man, and Cody wants to hear 'em. Let's put 'em down." He was already nodding to Cody when I said no.

"Not tonight."

"What're you fuckin' crazy? You fucked up. This is absolutely the right time for this, Ray . . ."

I looked past him at Reggie. She met my eyes and smiled without blinking, Cody talking to her, Lonnie talking to me, and they couldn't see it, the intention between us, naked and glowing and so easy I laughed.

"You think it's fuckin' funny, man? I'm talkin' up your shit an' you think it's fucking funny," Lonnie bitched.

"I don't want to play my music here," I explained. "It's not ready." Reggie and Cody had joined us. Lonnie was putting on an act of some kind, like he was insulted beyond belief. I faced Cody and shrugged. "I think I write some good music," I said straight. "I like doing it, but it's not ready, and . . . and I don't know you. I don't trust you."

He laughed out of embarrassment. "I can dig that."

"Nothing personal."

"That's good, Ray. I like that." But he was lying, he didn't like it from me at all.

Lonnie was stunned into numb silence. Reggie could not take her eyes off my face, her grinning shock embarrassed me before Cody, and he thought I was awkward because of him.

"Let me explain," I offered.

"It's cool, Ray. When you're comfortable, man." Cody's sense of power rebounded quickly, his ego was too great to accept insult for long. "I understand completely," he said.

"I write for myself, Cody," I stopped him with my hand. "I'm not just along for the ride."

"Nobody said you were, man." Again he laughed without heart. "But we can try something I got in mind. Dancer, check this," and Cody wrapped his arm around the kid's shoulder, huddled over a list of songs.

"Smooth," Lonnie mumbled.

I felt her looking at me and finally raised my eyes to her big-ass grin. "Did you ever think of bein' a salesman? You know, Ray the Face, selling things? Washers an' dryers, TVs, cars, or maybe community service? You're so good with people," she said flatly, and walked away.

It took Jello half an hour to answer the door. I waited in the dark. I could hear music. The door was unusually small, like a cottage door at the top of the metal stairs. She lived in an apartment over the side alley where someone had planted a path of red bricks in the dirt. Looking down made me dizzy and suddenly out of breath.

Jello was nervous on the other side of the door; she laid a hand softly across her mouth. There was a thin glass window in the top of the door, but she didn't look out. She asked who it was twice.

I told her twice, "Ray the Face," but my voice didn't seem very proud of it. I was thinking about Reggie, about sleeping with her, about Lonnie lying beside her right now, his legs stretched out against hers, his hand resting on the curve of her naked back. I almost left then, I started to, when the door opened on a chain, and a strip of face purred a smile out at me. She was dressed in a deep-blue Japanese robe that couldn't've been very warm and white sweatsocks. And she looked great.

"Well looka' this shit," she said.

"You said breakfas' sometime."

"That was weeks ago. You're drunk, baby."

"Okay. I'm drunk." I fidgeted around; behind me sunrise was an hour away. "You're still up I see," I said.

"Ah-hmmm . . . jest windin' down after work." She opened the door. "An' you got no place else to go," she said, mocking me with her firm voice and tilted eyebrows. "It never works for anybody, no matt' what lies they gonna tell you." I just looked at her.

"I doan have my sunglasses," I finally said.

"You're a bad actor, RayBird." Jello yawned and hummed a little unconsciously, her kimono drifted apart enough to show me deep black thighs that prickled with gooseflesh. Her nipples were so hard under the silk, I couldn't look at them. And she was thinking, "Man, I got him."

And I was thinking, "Man, she's got me now."

"I don't have a thing to drink," she said as if that would be a problem.

I held out a six-pack in a brown bag. Jello was not about to let me come in for free, I knew that; it would cost a six-pack and a pint of my juice. She wasn't about to give it up like that, but she was laughing now, her throat bared and her head tossed back and she let me in. My saxophone stayed in the kitchen. On the floor by the garbage.

I bent down and pulled her panties off from under the robe before I had removed my jacket. She kissed me hard on the back of my neck. I wanted to take her standing up, but Jello had other ideas and for a moment the silence was heavy, awkward between us, then quickly we were in her bed. Her breasts were soft, flattened out like thick pancakes as she stretched out on her back, very black skin, the nipples large and blacker. Purple. I tried to touch her gently, to start slowly, helplessly, but I had never been so hard. The smell of her slipped up my nose and it stopped being me and it started being her. The whole game. Jello ran down the hydraulics of love, full oh-come-on, baby, oh-come-on stomach slamming to slow, full-body sensations. She was a work-horse, subtle as a soft ditch when the moments called for softness, a hard-thighed fucking obscene earthquake when the moments turned ripe. She came hanging from the towel rack in the shower, so much water running over her face and me straining to hold her there, and finally choking to a quit because Jello could not stop laughing. She'd drown first. I had not known this woman, who made love for fun. And it scared me a little that she was so good at it.

"You want some of this?" Jello asked, snuggling deep into the covers. The room was completely dark, heavy curtains against the daylight; her bedroom showed only outlines. She clicked on a lamp on the floor. Held out a clear vial of cocaine.

"No." I fell back into a pillow. I listened to her take two hits, and again Reggie floated back into my mind. I knew that Jello expected more, she wanted more. I wondered if Reggie was the same, or would she want to lie her head on my chest and sleep in the dawn?

"Here . . . I'll take a hit in my mouth." She handed me a cap full and I threw it back to my throat. A Bad Taste.

The glass window in the kitchen was fogged from the top down like a bathroom mirror; I got another beer, looked around the room vaguely wondering how it happened that I was here, standing here naked. I heard her click off the light. She was cuddled in the blankets, high, her arm cocked behind her head and a peaceful smile. Jello looking helpless. That made me laugh.

"What's so damn funny?"

"Nothin' . . ." I passed before the bed and crawled in, bed springs moaned, springs that I hadn't noticed before. "You want a sip of this?"

"Close the covers! You're lettin' the cold air in!"

"Nothing cold about this bed. Any cigarettes?"

And we passed the morning like this, cocaine, beer, cigarettes, all of it in the dark. I could see her now, my eyes adjusting, the room lightening. Her shadow on the pillow became a face with shadows of its own, under her lips, trailing her throat; and she was beautiful like this; she wasn't Allie or Reggie, she wasn't the one and she was beautiful. Black woman in white sheets. Contentment flushed high in her face, not the barmaid of the St. Charles Club, but I saw a woman with a soft name who knew she wasn't the one and didn't care.

"What're you starin' at? Is my nose runnin'?"

"No. I'm just lookin' at you."

But Jello pulled me down in the bed, strong-arming my head to the pillow next to hers, rumbling "baarumpha do-do-doo" along with the music, her jaw muscles jumping and grinding with the drug, and she kissed my eyes and laid back. I poked my head under the covers and laughed. "Smells like a can of worms in here," I told her.

"Yeah, I've been told I'm extremely . . ."

"Fertile?"

"I think the word is *juicy.*" She grabbed me and we played at it until she felt me coming around again, and her eyes grew soft-lidded and bright. "Did you really want breakfast, Ray?"

"Not really." I thought about it. "Can you really make eggs?"

"Honey, I can make eggs talk."

It wasn't as pretty then as before, as kind, or as friendly, but we fucked until it was over for good, and our bodies were gummy to the touch and her hair wasn't soft and sleek, but like steel wool bunched on her head. My arms hurt in the biceps where she'd held me, and my cock was red and dead-sore and the skin on my knees burned. Then Jello, with the confidence in character of the woman that she was, not some cast-off whore, coke freak, five-o'clock-fuck, got up and fried bacon and eggs, chopped mushrooms and peppers, cooked a dozen frozen-food French fries and we sat in bed and ate. Drank one last beer. And I fell asleep with ketchup on my mouth.

10

The old man moves easily down the sidewalk. The sun is very bright and he still insists on carrying the saxophone under his arm because he cannot bring himself to trust the paperclip handle. It is crowded. The city has by now been divided in half; one half is very rich and the streets are wide with concrete squares of trees and hedges lining the curbs, the buildings are walled off and policed by private guards. The old man lives in the other half, where the streets are narrow and jammed with the poor begging off the poor. There are two kinds of residents here; the very young in their rags of nonconformity, and the very old in their rags of poverty. The dressing is different for effect, as calculated as any military uniform claiming rank and performance, medals of conduct good and bad, identifying and separating at a glance. The old man wears a tie around his neck, the young man with the shaved head walking beside him wears a tie around his waist. The same tie. The same clothes of multiple ownership cut up and torn and draped and worn in different ways, sizes that fit. They don't know it, but the old man wishes he could paint his hair electric green and sport car key earrings, but he would look ridiculous and even older for it. And they find him in a way, they talk to him on a bus stop bench and always want to know, "Why would anyone live that long? Why would anyone *want to?*" He tells them it happens that way. Not important except that this is where the old man lives, in the shared half of a divided city.

He works the first phone booth on his circuit. He takes a short piece of copper wire with a hook bent in the end from his pocket and hides it in the palm of his hand. He looks around the street; the sidewalk is busy and moving quickly by him. There is a barefoot bum going through the garbage cans piled on the corner, and the old man thinks, what one man throws out, another man can use, and the bum finds a red child's cap that he tries on his head, and a plastic bottle of prescription pills, and the old man watches with interest as the bum works the top off and takes a few capsules with a casual fuck-it, it can't hurt me either way, and a couple of ballpoint pens that won't write, but he takes them anyway.

No one is watching the old man as he inserts the hooked wire up the coin return slot of the pay phone and carefully removes a wadded white cloth. Behind the cloth a handful of quarters and dimes clatter into the coin return dish. He takes the money and the wire into his pockets and replaces the white cloth for harvesting tomorrow. He is the ultra-modern trapper of the American city and he moves on with his eye already focused on the next phone booth down the street; he runs a line of ten in this neighborhood, makes about twelve dollars a day. He used to run a lot more and he smiles to himself thinking about all the walking.

"Get the fuck out of the way, old man." The punk is a big boy with huge arms and ominous tattoos. He brushes harshly past, then turns. "You think you own the whole fucking sidewalk."

"Okay, okay." He grips the saxophone case, wanders to the curb.

He lets them get far away, then works his phones.

At the Greek diner the food is very cheap and he sits at the counter; the waiter is dark, a beefy face and eyes like a bull, a mustache so stiff it seems frozen to his lip.

The old man gives him his best grandfatherly smile.

"Let me guess, huh?" says the counterman. "You think you wann haf two eggs over easy, hash browns, no sausage, no bacon, but a small herring in cream sauce, because somabody tolds you it good for your heart. Right?"

"It is, it is, the arteries. And . . ."

"And a beer."

"A bottle of beer," corrects the old man, "because . . ."

"Because out of a can you no like it."

"No, I don't like that. Tastes like dirt. And a glass of water when you can get it."

"Oh, I can get it," and the dark man grins. "Old man," he says, "don't you ever get tired of this? All the time this same thing every day?" He serves the glass of water.

"No." The old man wets his mouth. "There was a time, you could never believe it—I don't blame you for turning your face—I had champagne and women for breakfast, every day. All kinds and sizes and colors of women."

"Ahhh, you guys all big shits, hey."

"It wasn't any different than this, my friend, no different. And I refuse to give the slightest fuck about it anymore."

The waiter slides down the counter toward the grill and the old man slowly counts out his pocket full of change, stacking the quarters in one pile, the dimes and nickels in another.

11

Reggie let me in. It was after noon; I hadn't called, I had made no plans with her, but impulsively showed myself at her door. She looked down at the sax case, her eyes wide and wiseass. The dim shock on her face passed to an air of quiet radiance, to an even more reckless curiosity. She had her hair tied back and no makeup, her lips were a wonderful bloodless color like a soft bronze. She was barefoot. Reggie almost made a sound, almost squeaked something feminine, but she covered her mouth with two fingers and simply stepped aside in the doorway. I slipped inside trying to ignore the thrill of the closeness to her body.

"I want to show you a few things," I said, taking off my jacket, and did not wait for her answer, but placed my case on the table and began unzipping the sax.

"How did you know I was home?" she asked facing me.

"I didn't." I stopped with a sudden thought. "Are you doing anything, I mean . . ."

She walked to her window and looked out. "You are really something, man." She wasn't smiling and there was no friendliness in her voice; she was deciding.

I just started to play.

It must have been thirty minutes, longer. I played five songs before she stopped me.

"Has anyone else heard this?" she asked very quietly.

"No. Just you. Lonnie's heard bits an' pieces."

"Have you written out any of it?"

"Yeah. Here are the sheets." I took them from my case and passed them over to her. Reggie straightened them out with her hands, smoothing them flat, pulling at the corners. "This is how you carry your precious music 'round? Looks like some third-grade homework. Is it all here?"

I looked over her shoulder at the crumpled pages. "Yeah . . . I think so." I felt I had played it poorly, unemotionally, technically, mechanically, but without the heart. Or the fierce impulse that drove me, without the tension or the anger or the fear this music demanded of me. That was the way it was written, full of doubt and promise. "I play it better when I'm alone," I told her.

Reggie laughed. "Why are you layin' this . . . this presentation on me, Ray the Face? I didn't think you trusted people."

"Work with me." I shouted at her, not realizing I held my hand out, then seeing it and feeling stupid, "Just work with me," I said.

"Me?" She was laughing at herself, tentatively, but with great calculation she was running the possibilities, coldly, running the word through her mind. "Ray, I have nothing . . ."

"Don't bullshit me, Reggie, an' don't walk to the window." I stopped her and she wheeled with a violent passion in her face, shooting from her eyes, trying to kill me. "The music needs a voice . . . the horn isn't enough," I said.

"Lyrics?" She asked herself the question and sat back on her nice couch. She played with her fingers and looked up at me through her lashes. "Maybe we should just talk a lit'le . . . we have to find out . . ."

"It's all about the same thing," I explained, moving about the room without seeing it, only her, and then I couldn't remember later what she was wearing. "It's the same theme over an' over. It's street crime. It's about money. Money an' crime. Reggie, it's supposed to be violent."

"It is."

She worked on the songs differently than I would. I attacked them all as one tangled piece of material, prying individual riffs and melodies apart, mixing all the sheets together on the floor and building them from there, like a collage, or a musical puzzle, deciding which pieces locked together, which were the blue sky, which were the ocean white caps. Reggie took each song as a final product, as an end, an accomplishment in itself. She hung the sheets on a corkboard panel in her kitchen and scribbled on them in thick pencil. She kept everything at eye level and danced about the apartment singing to herself. At first she experimented with a Sony cassette tape recorder, but found that it only slowed her down. I sprawled the sheets over the counter and played the sax in tiny breaths, but mostly I just watched her, carefully noting the way she assembled the music; she fit the pieces as I would have, only she was much more delicate; her influence was the best measured in the quality of the tone. Like taming the animal.

She worked very hard at it. I was right about that. I had guessed that she would concentrate. I had guessed that Reggie wanted it as badly as I did. We both turned to the sound of a key in the door; she turned to the clock, it was after six. "Shit," she said glancing strangely at me.

Cody came in carrying his briefcase, dropping his keys on the table. I fired her a quick, questioning look, but found nothing in the split second of her eyes; she revealed nothing. But Cody had a wild look of astonishment that he could not keep off his face. He stared at me, then at her. We were in the kitchen. Then came the mocking grin, the fake laugh. "Hey, what's gonna' on Ray the Face," he said, and took my hand. Cody kissed Reggie on the cheek, called her baby.

"We're workin' on Ray's music," she said pointing to the board. Cody moved to it, ran his eyes over the sheets.

"No titles?" he asked.

I shook my head, but didn't speak, I could feel myself giving away the shock of him there, his keys on the table, his ease in her apartment.

"Titles are important, you know. It's the first thing the public sees, it's the first thing the producer sees, right there on the top of the page. Before he hears one single note. Writers have a tendency not to think about titles." That was all he said about the music. He opened a cabinet and poured a glass of cold vodka from the freezer. He offered me one, but again I just shook my head.

"I have to go. I didn't know it was so late." I started to gather the sheets together. Reggie watched me and seemed uncomfortable as if she wanted to say something, but didn't know what. As if she wanted to explain.

"Cody, the stuff is fresh, it's workable. I mean it's very workable." She looked at me as if I was going to thank her but then realized I wasn't interested, I was watching Cody's face, and he wasn't interested either. He was wondering what I was doing in their apartment. And I was asking myself how stupid I could be not to have seen it from the very beginning.

"Well . . . maybe someday I get to hear it," and again he laughed, but didn't mean it.

Reggie walked me to the door. It was dark out now, the outlines of the trees were kindly haunting, softly edged and the air was cold. Reggie's eyes had a sudden brightness, a black courage.

"Ray, you got to get over him." she tapped her hand against my sax case. "What's in here is too important. It's important to me. I want to keep doing it."

"Okay." I was flattered in a second-hand way. "Thanks," I said indifferently. "Reggie, where does Lonnie fit into all of this?"

"I don't know. Does he fit in at all?" she asked back.

I liked walking home in the cold streets. I had not thought about Reggie's apartment when I was there, the furniture or Indian rugs on the walls, the expensive lamps and the framed photographs in the hallway. Now I was thinking about it all. How did she afford it? It was too nice. She was taking it from Cody and I had the feeling he didn't matter any more or any less than the next guy; she was going to get to the top. She would take it from anyone. I laughed. Reggie too had solved the problem of money and art. She was a mugger like me. Like Lonnie. She did it with her legs. I had to laugh out loud.

It was dark enough. I was alone. An easy-rolling walk down the sidewalk, alone. Small, dark groceries, hand-painted wooden signs, the gates pulled closed over the fronts making steel diamond shadows on the doorways. Secured with old rusted padlocks the size of a fist. A neighborhood of homes, small, common homes with broken front walks, waist-high mesh fences, scratched paint and peeling roofs. Missing numbers by the doors. Little two-stories. Houses like the faces in a child's drawing book, a curl of smoke from the imaginary chimney, eyes from windows. I was toying with the idea of a solo, a purse snatch. It was dark enough.

I should have had a hat. There should be an alley to beat it down. I had staked out a bus stop across the street, knelt and pretended to tie my sneakers, eye hunting the street for an escape once they started screaming. I could come up from behind the concrete bench, select a victim and make the hit, take off like a crazed junkie and they would never see my face. But it was a long block. Dogs would be howling. The house directly behind the bus stop was backlit from within, yellow-green like swamp lights; the front window was open a foot to let the breeze in, the TV was loud enough to hear across the street. I studied the entire scene; the half moon spread a thin layer of silver over the street with some beauty, some menace. There was a taint of death in this planning; the black figures on the bench, the waiting silence before the struggle and sudden, bitter violence, and my body filled with chills and eyes glittering with the madness of my crime. I yawned again and again from nerves. Kept looking away as if the scene would change, let me go. Feel the death, whose death? I watched the house, imagined a fat-bellied old Mex padding out barefoot in a torn T-shirt to see what the hell all the screaming was about. Then closing the window. The neighborhood was careless, loose; the boundaries between the houses were varying stages of undergrowth, shaggy fan palms with thick, hairy trunks, wild oleander hedges with reddish flowers. Littered beer cans shining through the bushes. Cars parked over the sidewalk in weedy yards. High crime.

The only people riding the bus at that time of night were old, old women and Mexican mothers who sat without moving any more than it takes to inwardly pray their rosary. I stalked them. My unshadowed stare gave way to a flickering smile. "What the fuck am I doing?" I said softly to myself. Hearing my voice an old woman jerked to face me. She dropped the change in her hand, it scattered across the curb.

"Let me get that," I knelt to retrieve her coins.

"You startled me," she said.

"I . . . I . . . I didn't mean to scare you." I handed her the bus fare.

"My transfer. I've lost my transfer." She searched her lap.

I found the slip of paper on the ground and handed it to her without looking into her face.

"Thank you, young man."

I could feel her staring at my back as I hurried away, "What the fuck am I doing?" And the only answer was I had no idea.

We hit a man in a phone booth, again after sunset, but not late, maybe around nine. He was young, a preppie or yuppie or a good fake, three-piece suit, tassled Loafers, perfect haircut and tan, a total picture of how to dress for success. It sounded like he was talking to a girl on the phone, setting something up, a phony laugh and a cocky attitude. He was playing pocket pool with his change, looking down at his watch. Lonnie hit him from behind, drove his face into the phone box so hard his nose started to bleed instantly. Broke it open across the bridge. He tried to fight; Lonnie cracked his head again and he quit, held up his hands. I stuck the mouthpiece from my horn in his back like it was a knife. "Okay . . . okay," he said hoarsely. I went through his pockets and Lonnie and I said nothing at all. I took everything and stuffed it into my jacket. "Keep your face on the phone, Pork," Lonnie rasped into his ear, and we were gone.

The vic had a solid-gold pen, about eighty credit cards, and thirteen dollars in cash.

"Man, this is horseshit," Lonnie spit out the car window. "Can't fuckin' believe it."

"That shit's gonna happen," I shrugged.

"That shit doesn't happen if you know what you're doin'."

"It's experience, you know, a learn-through-doing kind of job." I laughed. "That's a joke, Lon."

"This is the joke, RayBird. Takin' off these fuckin' dudes. Small time, we're thinking strictly small time." He kept shaking his head.

"Hey man, don't forget why we're doing this in the first place. To keep making music. Don't forget it. This is not the end. It's only a means . . . to keep us alive . . . to keep us playing . . . creating." He wasn't listening to me. "I don't like what you're thinking."

"You can tell yourself anything you want to about what this is supposed to be 'bout. But it's jive, Ray. This is about money. An' I say if we're gonna do it, let's do it right. Let's not fuck around."

It was ten days before Christmas when we robbed a cab driver. There was nothing I could do about it. It was not my idea, but I could not stop Lonnie, so I put down with him. It didn't go quite as we had planned. Lonnie had some fucked-up notion that cab drivers have a lot of money in the front-seat cigar box. I said no-way, but if we were going to try a cab, our best chance would be to pick one out at the airport; the fares would be bigger anyway. I kept watching him as we searched for a place to park the car. I smoked cigarette after cigarette while Lon played with the radio, chatted about Reggie and Cody and some grand scheme for a record label. He asked me if things were any better with Allie. It was like we were on our way to a Lakers' game, just out for a drive. There was a cool confidence in his voice, in the touch of his hands on the wheel, in every little move he made, in his dark eyes checking the traffic. "This looks pretty good here." he said, "We'll take a cab to LAX, head 'em out this way, hit 'im and make it across the dark lot. Okay?"

"Okay." I wondered again what the fuck I was doing, but it was already too late; Lonnie had made the change, he wasn't even nervous about it any more. I could see it in him so clearly that I wondered also, was it happening to me?

Lon reached under the seat and came up with a gun, a small black revolver with a deep-purple plastic grip.

"What the fuck is that shit?" I dropped my hand heavily on his arm.

"It's Keeber's. He won't miss it."

"No, Lon, no man, no, no, no, no, no."

"It's not loaded, Ray. Jesus, man, you think I'm crazy?" He showed me the empty cylinders, clicked down the hammer on the empty chamber. It was a sudden, sickening, flat sound.

"No, Lon, this is gettin' out of hand."

"C'mon, Ray. These guys carry baseball bats, shit like that. What're supposed to take 'im off with my thumb? It's just for show, scare 'im a little so he does what we want." He placed the gun on the seat between us, kept talking in a voice so matter-of-fact that it frightened me more than the weapon. "It's to make sure that nothing goes wrong. Insurance, baby. We don't want to get hurt either, you dig?"

"It stays in the car." I took it off the seat before he could stop me. "Give me the keys. I'm puttin' this thing in the trunk."

He gave me the keys and I hid it under the spare tire, stuffed rags around it. Lonnie watched me with a curiously untroubled look on his face, almost a smirk, as if he had been just teasing me, a trial run. See what I would do.

The driver shot us the big-eye over the seat back. "Any luggage?" he asked in a suspicious tone that gave me the chills. I had a bad feeling about this instantly and it just kept getting worse.

"Motherfuckers lost it, man . . . you believe that shit?" Lonnie swore, pointing through the glass door at the airline counter, "Don't fly fuckin' Continental, baby . . . they don't know their ass from their elbow." He grinned now, easily. So easy, this lie slipped from his mouth like a kiss. The driver relaxed, laughed. Lonnie gave him the fake address in El Segundo and winked at me.

"It's not cool," I whispered at him.

Lonnie frowned, tightened his fist on the seat. Yeah, yeah. He mouthed the words at me, gestured for me just to sit back.

I shook my head. "It's not cool," I said softly.

He caught the driver's eyes in the rear view and continued his ad lib. "Goddamn right it's not fuckin' cool. I gotta buy some new underwear." And Lonnie kept the driver happy all the way to the top of a small hill, then he pulled a three-inch piece of copper pipe from inside his jacket and pressed it quickly against the back of the driver's skull. There was no way for him to see it, he only felt the cold round metal O."

"This is a rip," Lonnie started.

But before he could finish, the driver screamed and spit-flew and he didn't stop to look back at anything; his reaction was instant and one motion, he jumped. It happened so quickly all I saw was the door hanging open like an elephant's ear and Lonnie holding a piece of copper pipe in the air; the driver was gone, rolling away twice in the street. And in that instant the cab was gaining speed on the hill, steering itself across the lane toward a wire fence and a ditch filled with garbage. I could see that much in the headlights, nothing beyond it.

Lonnie froze on me and there was no time. I was halfway over the front seat, reaching for the wheel, when we hit the fence, through it with a long wrenching rush of metal and bumped to a jolt in the ditch. I landed face first on the floor staring at the gas pedal; my ear was bleeding where it hit the dash but I could hear the keys dangling in the steering column and turned off the engine. Lonnie had the door open and was trying to get me out, pulling to free my shoulders. "I'm okay . . . I'm okay," I said, but I couldn't back up and had to let him pull me out head first through the door.

"Shit, Holy Fuck, Ray!" Lonnie was wide-eyed, holding me by the arms. I must have looked a mess, because he was afraid. "RayBird, Ray Bird . . ." was all I heard.

The money had spilled from the cigar box on the floor. I picked as many bills as possible before the haze cleared and the fear mounted in its place, Lonnie pulling at me, pulling to get away and fuck the money. But I got as many bills as possible. And then we ran, Lonnie holding me up across the dark lot.

I topped the second flight of stairs to our apartment; my body was aching all over. My ear had stopped bleeding but it felt like a foot on the side of my face. The air in the short hallway was hot and claustrophobic, a musty darkness that never saw the sun. The windows were nailed shut against burglars. I kicked into a suitcase with my foot, almost fell, caught myself and looked down. There were two old suitcases and a soft dufflebag in front of the door. And they were mine. I found the note taped to the door:

"Ray, the locks have been changed. I am with friends and out of town for a few days. Don't get crazy, Ray. I told Janis to call the police if you throw a fit, and she will. I told the landlord you no longer live here. You can pick up the rest later."

It was signed, then scratched out in afterthought. She didn't even say she was sorry. Not one kind word. I tried my keys and knocked a hundred times. I hadn't imagined that it would happen this fast. I had thought that Allie almost enjoyed the fighting, I had thought the wild musician ol' man rounded out her experience the same way people work at jobs they hate and don't know why. I hadn't seen it; what was clear to all her pals at work, what was clear to Lonnie. But I wasn't that surprised, no, not that surprised. I thought of her sleeping with a lawyer somewhere, curled up naked next to him gently in the dark, and even though it was only a matter of time, and even though birds of a feather eventually sleep together, it bothered the shit out of me. But I wasn't that surprised, and no sense kicking in the door if you're not that kind of guy. I sat down and waited, leaned back into the wall and began to miss her already.

12

He could see the St. Louis lights across the river. A dome of neon light the color of bone dropped in a black sky. Lights running like shiny legs on the water in front of him, rosy light on the Mississippi. Easing into the mud banks. All the way across the river, the lights stopped at his feet, right off the tip of his tennis shoes. It was adult light and he knew it. He had a few more swallows of beer and tried to focus on Stan telling some nigger story, but Ray could only see him through one eye and he was sure he had already heard the story a hundred times.

". . . an' we had three of these air pump kinda BB guns. Those little fuckers really sting! Really." Stan picked up a stick and pretended he was sighting down the barrel, laughing and spitting through his teeth. Whenever he was excited he spit all over.

"Really, lit'le fuckers," Brillo butted in, "my fuckin' ol' man won't let me get one of those."

"C'mon, Brillo, I'm tellin' a goddamn story."

"Yeah, Brillo, shit. You can't drink worth a shit," said Knots. He opened a can of Bud. "Let's see you chug this, you chicken shit."

Ray put a hand on Brillo's back to keep him from falling

over. Head back, he threw it down. On the embankment above them a single car gunned it up the River Road, moving fast enough to fantail gravel and summer dust. In the cone of the headlights Ray could see Brillo's face, sweaty and burned pink, his eyes filmy and mechanical.

"So what was I talkin' about? Oh, yeah, we got these three air-pump guns . . ."

"The lit'le fucks really zing." Knots sat on a rock watching Stan and grinning like a wino.

"An' Ralph's Mustang," Stan spit, "four-speed Hurst in it. Sonofabitch's faster 'n greased shit. We cruise down through East St. Louis nigger town. See a buncha dumb fuckin' niggers fuckin' off on a corner, an' Pow! Pow! Pow! Pow! See them niggers jumpin' 'round like . . ."

"Oh, fuck." Ray held Brillo's head up, but it was way too late.

"Jesus Christ, man, he's tossin' his cookies."

"Can't drink worth a shit," said Knots. He opened another beer. "When he's done, give him this. It's the best thing. That's what my old man does."

Brillo fell back against the bank wheezing like an old dog that can't catch its breath. He tried blowing his nose through two fingers, but only gagged himself back into the dry heaves. Ray picked him up. "Jesus, Brillo, real neat. Here, drink a few slugs. Get that shit outta your throat. You puked all over your shirt."

"Gross, man," laughed Stan. "Gross."

They called the band The Mystery Trend and Knots was the oldest member, almost nineteen, out of school for two years now, they were his band, he called the shots. There weren't that many to call. Their "repertoire" consisted of nine songs down to memory, the slow numbers were all Beatles, the rock cuts were all Stones and The Birds, but the kids didn't seem to mind. They didn't even notice half the time, Ray would stretch "Get Off My Cloud," the biggest request and a kind of informal theme song with them, into a nice, long, sax solo cut in the middle until the bunnies had no idea what they were playing anymore. They could start the next set with it. Over an' over. Knots had arranged the sets to get them all hot and sweaty with three straight high-energy numbers, then glue them together with two drowsy Beatle tunes, clinging around the hall in the first feel of the night. The boys pull the shirttails out to cover slowdance hard-ons. They didn't care if we only knew nine songs. They just wanted to dance and drink beers from milk cartons out behind the gym. Especially the Catholic kids, man, they never got a chance during the week. Friday night was important. Critical. Catholic kids danced while they did sound check.

Brillo was probably the best musician, electric bass, strong chord work, and he could follow anybody into anything, but he was such a queer no one cut him any slack; he couldn't make it. Stan made a ton of noise on the drums; he was limited to one speed, 4/4 no matter what. Ray's father heard them rehearse in the basement, "The only thing Stan knows about a beat is that it's a vegetable," he'd said. Knots was the sex star, lead singer and guitar, and he was good up front. Ray could see him in Las Vegas someday; his guitar sucked gas, but the chicks loved him. Ray filled in the gaps.

He packed up the sax, Knots walked over to the bandstand with the money; the gym was empty except for the geeks on the dance committee, up on ladders, taking down decorations, everybody was outside in the parking lot, cooling off.

"These priests are weird, man," said Knots. His long hair was soaking wet. "They act like they're ashamed to hafta pay the band or somethin'. Weird. They put the cash in a white envelope an' kinda slip it into your hand like . . ."

"Maybe they're just used to gettin' their money in envelopes," Ray laughed, but only Brillo laughed with him. Knots had no idea what he was talking about.

"Yeah, maybe, I guess."

"How much?" Stan had his hand out.

"Eight bucks apiece." And before Stan could bitch Knots added, "I gotta pay for the mikes an' shit, you know."

"Okay, let's get some booze," said Stan.

"With what?" whined Brillo. "Let's get outta here."

"Chip in two bucks. I'll use my ID."

"Let's ride down to the river an' cool off, man."

"Tits."

"That thing's a piece a' shit, Stan," Ray took his ID from his shirt pocket. "It says you're supposed to be twenty-six for fuck's sake."

"Too much."

"Hey, I could pass for twenty-six."

"Really. No problem, Stan."

"C'mon, we gotta try something." Knots handed each of us our eight dollars. "Everybody throw in two bucks."

Ray humped Brillo up on a rock by the bank, his shoes were still in the river; he splashed water on Brillo's face, Brillo gone lumpy and white, tried to act tough, drinking from the can, coughing up grunts and hacks.

"Give me a cigarette," he said.

"Betcha I can piss all the way to the river," shouted Knots behind them in the dark. Their faces were moving on Ray, swaying white cheeks, drunken smiles, he could hardly see them.

"No fuckin' way." Stan unzipped his pants. " 'amn, you got an ugly pecker. Like a Falstaff stubby."

They lined up on the rocks, squeezing their dicks to make a piss arch forward through the night, thudding little puddles in the mud.

"If it's white it's all right," crooned Stan. Brillo fell off backward, spilling beer on his pants. Ray opened another can. The beer and urine and catfish mixed smells in the warm breeze, a long empty whistle out on the river, the waves hush-hushed, nobody 'round here goin' anywhere. Ray let himself drift.

"Who the fuck is that?" Stan yelled suddenly. He tugged at his pants and said, "Aw shit." Then they could hear giggles and gagged laughter and rocks sliding down the embankment. Knots jumped behind a short stand of pussywillows, his jeans caught down around his knees. Brillo didn't move a muscle.

"Far out. Can we bum a couple a' beers, you guys?"

Ray didn't know these two girls, but he knew about them, he didn't know their names. They went to Alton High, the same public school as Knots. They had been to the dance, hanging around the stage, not really dancing with guys, more moving with the music. They were Knots' groupies.

"Too much." She was wearing bell-bottoms cut low over the hips, a blouse tied up showing her belly button, her hair long, straight, parted down the middle, plastic bracelets rattled as she pointed at Brillo. "Wow, man, is he dead or something?"

"Was he ever alive?" Knots stepped into the clearing, he combed his hair back from his face.

"Oh, hi, Knots. Didn't know *you* were here."

"Yeah, sure." He made a move to give her a hug, easily dropping his arm about her waist, but she spun out before Knots could really touch her, a smooth, quick, dancelike turn that left him standing there with his arm out. Ray didn't know why it made him feel awkward, like something he couldn't see.

"Too much, man, you and Stan." She covered her face.

"Real funny." Stan, his back turned, still fought his zipper.

"Hi, sax man," Another pirouette, and she was facing Ray. He looked down at her feet.

"I like your moccasins," he said aloud.

"Yeah, my dad brought them back from Arizona." She lifted one foot to show him the beaded fringe in the back.

"That's Ray. He plays the sax in . . ."

She turned on Knots. "Really? No kidding, Knots." Then back to Ray. "I'm Glow."

"Glow?"

"Yeah, everybody calls me Glow." She danced away, then quickly said, "You play real groovy."

It was always the same with girls; one pretty one, one ugly one. A great unwritten plan of feminine instinct protected them both, the pretty one from the early stages of fear, free to flirt, and show off her belly button on a hot river night with drunken boys, the ugly one traveled with a passport of beautiful association. She wasn't that ugly, except for her fake laughter and her little piano legs. But it was a cheap trick. Stan and Knots ate it up. Starving. Ray sat on his rock next to Brillo and drank, watching them, impossible to believe that Stan could make a bigger asshole out of himself just because girls were around. He told the nigger story again; this time the Mustang was a Corvette. Glow smiled at Ray. He could barely see her.

"Why are you so mad?" Hand on hip like lightning before him. "You always like this when you get drunk? Wow."

"I'm not mad." Because Glow was wild and Ray wasn't, not enough. "I doan think I'm mad."

"You ever try any of this?" She held out a rolled cigarette.

"What is it?"

"Jamaican."

"Oh, yeah, yeah." What was she talking about?

Glow took a short drag and passed it to him. He inhaled it through his nose, an old trick, and coughed immediately.

"God, don't be so greedy. Bogart." She took it back.

Ray thought he was going to throw up right there on her moccasins. What was she talking about?

"Jesus! I smell grass. Glow, you got grass?" And Knots was moving in on the rock next to him. "Damn, where'd you get this shit?"

"Too much isn't it? Twenty dollars a baggie."

"Twenty bucks? Jesus."

"It's real good." Glow smiled at Ray. "Too much, isn't it?"

They sat in a tight circle of rocks and smoked two joints. Ray knew he was smoking grass, but he didn't know what was supposed to happen; if it was going to make him feel any better, it wasn't working. He didn't feel anything but the beer belching up in his throat. The fat girl giggled at everything Stan said, Glow grabbed his thigh and squeezed it in both hands. "I'm soooo wrecked," she laughed. Knots lifted Brillo's head, forcing the cigarette between his lips; he groaned and smelled like cat puke. Ray laughed and felt stupid, drank beer but his can didn't seem any emptier than when he opened it. Stan fell off his rock. The fat girl went insane.

"What time is it?" Glow jumped up and did one of her spins. "How long have I been here?" Man, he had no idea. An hour?

"I've got another joint in the car. C'mon Ray." She pulled him up, shambling up the embankment to the River Road, his head dented like any other old beer can, but laughing nonsense, holding soft hands twisted together in the heat. He staggered into the car, stuck his hand in his pocket to dry it off, felt the five dollars he had left. And gave it to her.

"I don't know, the grass I guess," Ray mumbled. She held the bills like a little green fan.

"Too much, man." She stared at him.

"Okay, I'll take two bucks back." He slipped two bills back in his pockets. One long moment they stood looking at each other, her face first time seen in the light, open-shaped with high Indian cheekbones and thick schoolgirl brows, blue-irised popped eyes, nice tits. She got in the car.

"C'mon, get in." She turned on the radio. "We'll find out what time it is." The Doors. "Light My Fire." "Wow, I love this song." They sang along, her jumping up and down slapping drumbeats on the dash. Ray looked, there were no headlights on the road.

"What do you think of this, too much, huh?" She had opened her blouse slightly to point out a small butterfly tattoo high on her chest. "Starts off as a glow worm."

"Far out." She didn't have a bra on. "Is it real?"

"Not this one, really. But I'll get one over in St. Louis. I already know a guy. I just wanted to see how it looked before I got the real thing. Glow Butterfly."

Ray began kissing her. He pressed hard against her, her mouth opened, she tongued him, poking his cheeks and the roof of his mouth like eating a stale candy bar; it hurt a little. He had worked up a thumper a long time ago, when Glow first touched his leg. Her blouse was wide open, bare tits and out-of-sight little brown nipples, Ray hurt all over. Ached. The news came on the radio.

"Shit. It's one o'clock?" Glow was out of the car, the door open, the interior lights on. Ray stared into his own arm pit. "Patty. Patty!! It's one o'clock! Patty!" She yelled down the ditch. He sat up blinking. Her breath was still in the car. Patty scrambled up to the door before he could get out. "Nice to meet you," she said. Glow ran around to his side. "I'll see you at the next dance, Ray."

"Wait." He stopped her. "I thought you, I thought you were, you know, you and Knots."

"Knots!" She kissed him quick. "Me and Knots a thing! I like Knots, but I like you too. I gotta go. Now."

Glow's car tore off; she forgot to turn on the headlights.

Knots drove them home in his car. A gold Plymouth that would do eighty-five in the flat, with Brillo and Stan passed out in the back, they hit ninety on the River Road. The car fishtailed through a gravel turn where the railroad tracks crossed the road, skidded into an intersection where the black-top pavement led into town. Knots ran the stop sign. Ray was trying to remember where his sax case was.

"Knots, did I put the sax in the trunk?"

"Yeah, all that shit's in the trunk." They blasted by the high school bluish-blur and Ray stuck his head out the window in the warm rush of air thinking it would do some good. But he still had a cigarette in his mouth. The hot ash blew right up his nose.

"Stop the car!" He jerked all over the front seat and Knots hit the brakes. Stan slammed into the seat back like a bean bag. Ray blew his nose into his hand, jumped and screamed; Knots held his head back and poured a little beer down his nose. "What the fuck." It burned. He blew his nose and they started laughing, sat down on the curb laughing, laid back on the sidewalk laughing.

At Brillo's house the light was on. He still couldn't walk worth a shit; they dragged him up to the front porch and sat him on the steps. Knots slapped him a few times.

"Christ, Brillo, c'mon," Ray whispered. "We gotta get home, Brillo, c'mon, man."

"Somebody's comin' to the door. Split!!" Knots was halfway across the lawn, Ray dove in the front door and they took off. Poor Brillo. Jesus.

They started coasting, lights off, a half block from his house, landed without a sound under the neighbors milkwood tree; the street was dark without a breeze, a single street light on the corner sputtered bluish-white, the bulb going bad. The table lamp in the living room window was on in his house; she'd waited up, sitting in the chair with a magazine. Shit! He'd get grounded for sure.

"Knots, Glow."

"What a flakey chick, huh?" He kinda grinned without meaning to. "Here." He handed Ray the sax case from the trunk. "See ya later."

"Hey, you think we'll ever really play gigs in St. Louis?"

"No problem, Ray. All we need is a keyboard. By the end of the summer." He looked at Knots, remembering the time he told Ray, "If I live past nineteen, I won't care about the rest of it, the best was already over." His eyes sharpened, went strange, into a quirky smile, he punched Ray's arm. He never knew if he liked Knots or not. He revved the Plymouth and laid rubber halfway to the corner. Ray dove face down into the front lawn and crawled in behind the hedge. "Fucking asshole." But no one came to the window. No one opened the front door. And in the dirt under the hedge, an idea filtered into his mind; no way he would ever sneak past her, the best thing to do was walk right in and face her. With some incredible story. Ray ripped his shirt and rubbed dirt over his chest and face; with a thorny branch he cut the back of his hand until he had enough blood to dab under his nose. He was ready. He had been jumped. A fight after the dance.

He stumbled into the kitchen table. "It's just me," he called, running water in the sink; he held a wetted paper towel to his nose, staggered into the living room, one hand supporting him against the wall, head down. "Boy, you're not going to believe what happened to me." But she wasn't there. One shaded lamp on the corner end table, two cones of light on the ceiling and floor. Padding down the hallway in a repeated command performance, their bedroom door open, but she wasn't there either. And Ray stopped the bullshit; there wasn't a sound in the house, just a nerve in the center of his head like a tiny tail wagging, wide awake.

"Hello. Hey! Hi! Is anybody home? Mom? Georgia?"

He moved through the rooms of the house, turning on lights as he went in some late-night-detective way, looking for clues, for anything missing or out of place, calling again, "Hey! Hello!" He was back in the kitchen, alone.

"Well, all right!!" What a break! Back home late, drunk

and slipped in free as a bird. Undetected. Ray poured a big glass of apple juice and ate two peanut butter and cheese sandwiches. "Mom must be out tracking down the ol' man," he said aloud. "Quarter after two. Georgia, who in the hell knows where she is." He ate four chocolate chip cookies and took off his shoes and socks, took off his shirt, and wiped off the dirt with the dish rag.

He circled the first floor once more, turning off the lights, sipping the juice, so thirsty, dragging his clothes behind him. He had to cut the grass tomorrow. Fuck, he didn't want to do that, he hated it worse than anything, but at least with Dad and Mom out late no one would be banging on his door at eight o'clock. He'd do it in the afternoon. No problem. Do the trimming on Sunday. No problem. The light was on in their bathroom; Ray didn't remember turning it on. Better be safe, she'd be pissed if she thought he was nosin' around in her bathroom. Door's not supposed to be locked . . . then he didn't turn the light on. He knocked again. The knob was the easy kind with the little hole in the middle; he'd picked it before with a bobby pin, just push in the middle catch. He picked it again.

She was lying on her face in a thickish puddle of vomit . . .

"No, No. Nooooo!"

. . . her neck grotesquely twisted to one side so that the tendons all bunched together like little bumps running up and down, swelling from her shoulder. There was vomit everywhere . . .

"MOTHER!"

. . . on the toilet seat, the tile wall behind it, on her face, matted in her hair, dried and already cracking on her hands . . .

"God. Mother. Please!"

. . . she was barefoot, in her old terrycloth robe only, naked underneath, white as death, no blood at all, her body looked dead, as if the bones had all gone soft, been pulled out.

"Mom. Mom." Ray turned her over and shook her, calling in her face the same plea, "Mom." He wiped her face off with his hands. There was nothing. He laid her head back and straightened out the awful jerks in her back, her legs, placed her arms by her sides. Nothing.

"Breathe!! Goddamnit!! Oh, c'mon, please, C'MON." Ray grabbed handfuls of her hair and shook her head between his fists, harder and harder. And harder. A rumbling! He heard it, he heard it, her stomach. He put his ear to her naked belly. Rumblings! She was alive.

"Breathe, Mother. Please, breathe!" Ray opened her mouth and cleaned fingerfuls of vomit, wiped them on his pants. The mouth to mouth was awkward, he knew he was doing something wrong! Ray blew into it. He made sucking noises; her cheeks puffed in and out, but when he stopped she was not breathing. She should be breathing by now. He tilted back her head, held her tongue down with his own and blew into his mother's mouth. He pulled away quickly, began puking in the bathtub. He wouldn't remember anything else.

The rain was great. He liked tons of thunder and lightning, counting the seconds to see how far away it was hitting, water pouring off the roof so fast the gutters wouldn't hold it, a haunted nightmare-sheet of rain. Lightning. One thousand one, one thousand two, one thousand three, but he didn't hear the thunder. Must have missed it. He stood under the eave smoking one of Dad's Camels. Wet as a fucking duck. Thick night rain; he couldn't see the house across the street. But he could hear them inside, fighting. Fucking fighting. He peeked in the screen window, Dad in view behind the curtains; he's drunk on the couch, in his rumpled, black band suit, smoking, and part of Georgia, an arm wearing a house coat, standing in the corner, then moves out of view. He crouched down, didn't want Dad to see him.

"Give me the keys," he yells.

"Get out of my way," Mom's voice, close.

"Elaine. Give me the goddamn keys."

And Mom moves quickly across his sight; she is dressed in her long blue coat, her nurse's coat he thinks, and she is carrying a suitcase.

"Don't bother to pretend. You don't want me to stay here. None of you do." She is going for the door. His cigarette went out. Sizzled. Mom had forced her way onto the porch, Dad drunk, hanging half-in, half-out the doorway, Georgia's head peeping around his shoulder.

"Don't you touch me."

"All right. All right." He laughed. "If you want to leave me so damn bad, go ahead. Let's see you do it." He almost fell over then, catching himself, laughing. "Go ahead. I don't think you can do . . ."

"Let her go, Dad." Georgia pulled him back in. Ray walked out into the open as if he might do something about it, but no one seemed to notice him. Mom threw her suitcase in the car. She didn't see him until she looked in the rearview mirror. He stood behind the car in the rain.

"Ray."

"Why are you going?"

"Because I'm tired."

"What am I supposed to do, Mom?" he asked.

"Honey, I don't expect you to understand. Not now. Not like this. But please get out of my way."

"I can't let you go, Mom. I can't."

He laid down behind the back tires of the car, right in the mud, face up in the rain. She started the engine, Ray heard the gear shift clunk into reverse. He didn't move. He knew she wouldn't do it. He heard her crying; she shut the engine off, slammed the door. She stood over him, rain falling from her face and shoulders, looking funnier than shit. Ray gave her his fourteen-year-old grin.

"My own son. Why are you doing this to me? Why?"

"I'm sorry, Mom. I knew you were only faking it, you know?"

She ran in the house. He let the rain wash the mud off his back.

"Ray? Ray?" He looked up and saw Georgia leaning over him, rows of white fluorescent tube lights behind her head.

"Are you all right? Ray? Uncle Harold was talking to you. Didn't you . . ."

"That's Okay, Georgia. Let him sleep. He needs the rest." Harold stood next to her with that stupid white pipe in his hand.

"I wasn't sleeping." Ray sat up quickly on the hard wooden bench; someone must have taken the cushions, he thought. There were cushions before. He yawned. He stunk of beer, covered his mouth. He was in pain.

"Ray, do either of you have any idea where he could be?" asked Harold, so sincere he looked as if he had been crying.

"No, we don't know," Georgia answered. She sat next to Ray, her large shoulders rounded forward, her chest caved in, always ashamed of being so tall, big; she propped an elbow on each knee and twisted her hands between them.

"We don't know where he is," she said.

"Well, we'll find him, I'm sure. Just, just take it easy. There's no need to worry." Harold couldn't look at Ray. "Is there anything you want?"

"No." He could not believe it. He had forgotten all about her. Down the long aisle of the hospital wing, the floor shiny and smelling of ammonia wall to wall, the windows showed early light, violet, like molten metal cooling in the frames; people had gathered in the waiting lounge, haggard faces turned his way in silence, a mood of horror and anger. Even the nurses seemed to be tiptoeing around them. At the other end of the hall a plain black and white clock: 6:30. In three hours Ray had forgotten all about Mother. He drove Harold away with his eyes.

"Where the hell is he, Georgia? Where?"

"I don't know." She was crying. "He played somewhere."

A priest entered the waiting room through a side door; he shook hands with Harold's wife, then Harold, they embraced. The priest patted Harold on the back as he held him.

"What's he doin' here? Georgia. It's not that bad. She's not gonna die or anything. What's he doin' here?" Ray was standing up, pointing, they were all watching him, fish heads all turned, bottomless eyes; the priest smiled and began walking toward him. He ran down the hallway, stopped, and his legs shook under him.

Ray knew of two or three clubs, mostly Negro joints in Woodriver and East St. Louis, worn-out oblivion bars that stayed open past four. Dad told him about playing there for free drinks with anyone that walked up to the old wood stand-up Baldwin and sat down. He phoned them but no one answered. They had all gone home. Gone somewhere.

He appeared at the end of the hallway. Georgia nudged Ray's elbow. He saw him, he could *feel* him coming. The relatives stiffened, turned their backs, assuming the look of church people. Harold knocked his pipe out in the ashtray, loading his gun. He was ragged drunk and completely beaten down with the news, walking slowly, carrying the sax case at his side, one hand stuck in his pocket, a gaunt, seamed face, like a man deep in lonely thought, but Ray knew better. He was just drunk. Georgia stood as if she might run to him, but something in his manner stopped her cold. He walked to them.

"Where is your mother?"

Georgia pointed to the door behind them; he dropped the sax case in Ray's hand and quietly went in.

Ray thought he would never come out, maybe he was sleeping in the chair next to her bed. An hour passed, maybe the doctor had given him something to calm him down. An hour and a half, the nurses checked in and out at regular intervals. They would not let them in. Georgia drank coffee and talked with the relatives. She was the star of the show. They left Ray alone. He was eating M & M's when Dad came out. He had been crying.

"Jim? Jim, is Elaine . . ." but he walked right through Harold's outstretched arm, ignoring him, lighting a cigarette without looking at any of them.

"Is she okay, Dad?" Georgia took his arm. He sat down next to Ray, exhaled smoke.

"Your mother," his eyes terrified. "She looks like a ghost. She doesn't want you to see her right now. In a little while . . . tonight. She's not going to die, okay. Weak as hell, groggy, but she will be all right." Georgia cried softly on Dad's shoulder. Ray didn't know, just didn't know. He stared at the M & M's melting together in his sweaty hand, and he continued slowly, "You probably saved her life, Ray, you an' her faith. After taking the pills she realized that God would not forgive her for what she was doing to us, her family. And she vomited. She forced herself. But she had taken too many. She would have died because no one was home, because I wasn't at home." He looked up at Harold. Dad had given him what he wanted. "Let's go someplace where we can talk." And he took them, Georgia and Ray, by the hand and led them down the hall. At the vending machine he bought coffee, got them each something, and they sat alone, Georgia, Dad, and Ray.

*   *   *

Ray was alone in the living room watching TV; somebody knocked at the front door.

"I got it," he called, peeked through the window. A strange guy, not much older than him, had a checked sport coat and white buck shoes. Jesus.

"If you're sellin' somethin', you're at the wrong house," Ray said, looking past him at the green Volkswagon parked in front of the house.

"No, no, I'm not selling anything. Are you James Miles?"

"That's my dad."

"Would you tell him I've come about the ad in the paper."

"What'er you talkin' about?" He took a newspaper page from his pocket. "What ad in the paper?"

"Right here, pal," he said, pointing. " 'For Sale. Used tenor saxophone. Selma. Very good condition.' This is 314 Jefferson Street, isn't it?"

"Let me see that." Ray couldn't believe his fucking eyes, his address? "No, no, there's some kinda mistake, pal." He put his hand on the door. "There ain't no saxophone here like that."

Dad walked into the living room rolling up his sleeves, an unopened beer in his hand.

"What's this, Ray?" He moved to the door. "Hey, can I help you, buddy?"

"Mr. Miles?"

"Yeah. Oh, you saw the ad."

"Yes, sir," the queer talked around Ray. "I'm here about the saxophone. If there's been some mistake."

"Naw, no mistake." Dad caught Ray's eye. "C'mon in. I'll get it for ya."

He sat and watched his dad sell it, throw in the case. Ray didn't believe it until that guy put his lips on the horn.

13

I don't know when it happened, but I turned cold. Turned cold to all of it. Fuckin' Christmas. Maybe it was when Allie came to the liquor store:

I moved across the storeroom to the back of the beer coolers. Through the glass front I could see her standing by the magazine rack, running her hand lightly over a few covers. She was smoking a cigarette and that was like her.

"Fuck, man."

Lonnie laughed in his throat. He stood beside me and peeked out at her. "Had to happen, baby," he smiled.

She was wearing her old jeans. Flat black shoes with crepe soles, the jeans fit tight as if she had just washed them. She had on a hooded windbreaker, light blue, L.L. Bean sailing clothes. She looked good, maybe a little too thin. Like she was still in college, up all night, no time to eat. Very popular, busy all the time, always running with a pack of girls who all looked the same, who were going in the same direction. She pretended not to hear my footsteps coming up behind her, the cigarette hand shot to her mouth, the other hand played in her soft blond hair as if it were trying to hide there.

And I was struck by how young she still seemed. I had

lived with her for two years and, now walking slowly up to her back, never realized how small she was. Her butt's no bigger than a banjo, I thought to myself. I stopped yards away from her.

"L.A. has a lot of dirty magazines, doesn't it?" Allie said without facing me. She returned a porno monthly to the rack. "Where do they all come from? God."

"Keeber's got most of them. I guess they go with the booze." I glanced around to see if they were watching me from the back. "How you been?"

She turned around quickly like it was some kind of surprise; she laughed a nervous sputter, and held her hand to her mouth, grinning behind it. Her face was bright with afterglow of the first day in the sun, intelligent and intent on giving nothing away. Her eyes, dry, large blue and bullheaded. She had sand and dried salt spray stuck to her bangs and she was very pretty.

"I want a bottle of rum. Can you sell it to me?" she said.

"Sure." I moved behind the counter. "Light or dark?"

"I don't care. A good rum, though."

I sold her the bottle, made the change, her hand was warm when I barely touched her.

"You won't be coming back, will you, Ray?"

"You don't want me to."

"But you're not going to try." Allie opened the bottle with a tender crack of the seal and drank a swig or two from the neck.

"You can't do that in here." I laid my hand on her arm, she offered me the bottle. "No, I don't want any."

She shook me off and drank again, already drunk. "You're going to stay here?" she asked after a moment of glaring around the store. "Get your old room back?" She was mocking me.

"Until I get some money together. They're good to me."

"They're just like you, or you're just like them."

"Let's take this outside." I came out from the counter.

"I don't want to embarrass you." She laughed. "I remember the first time you brought me here, drunker than this." Neither one of us said anything, or moved toward the door. And I saw a car with other couples in it outside the front window, waiting for her.

"You look like you expect me to cry."

"No, Allie, I don't."

"I missed you for a week," she interrupted, "one week. I just had to see how you were doing, who was paying for you this time. You're back where I met you, Ray. Doesn't that say somethin' to you?" She frowned and wiped hair away from her face; she was beginning to make a fool of herself and it was time to go. Go to the party.

"I missed you too, Allie," I said.

"You still have things at the apartment." She was moving toward the door, her back to him, swaying and holding the bottle to her chest.

"I don't need any of that stuff. You can just throw it all out," I called to her.

"I already did," she called back.

I watched her climb into the front seat of the car; they were all laughing.

And maybe it was when I caught Lonnie stealing from Keeber:

"What're you doin', Lon?"

The liquor store was empty after a busy Friday payday afternoon, six-packs and half-pints. I saw Lonnie behind the counter.

"What're you doin', man?" In the darkness outside, through the windows like a stage drop behind him, cars began turning on their headlights.

"Ah do this all the time . . . since Ah could first reach up to the box." Lonnie counted out money from the open cash register, folded it into his pocket. "Doan worry yo'self, Face."

"How much you take?"

"Jest what I need." Lonnie shrugged it off. "Ain't your business now, is it? Keeber knows."

"Okay."

Lonnie slammed the register closed, held the money in my face like a bouquet of weapons. "Look, bro, Ah got forty bucks here an' I got to have it." He went past me. "All Ah been doin' is wastin' my whole life takin' care of you, nigger, so I doan wanna hear no shit from you 'bout it. You got a free room, free time. Go write some more music. Cool." He left.

He was going to see Reggie. No doubt about it. Flashin' forty dollars on her, how stupid could he be?

And maybe it was Reggie that was turning me cold. She could do it. She called me now when Cody was gone from the apartment. We had an excuse. We had the music. We knew exactly what we were doing; we kept that rippling edge between us now by not letting it happen. The spell of sex. We knew whoever moved first was lost. Whoever falls in love loses. The only power is in not caring. Whoever cares loses. So we spent our days in a ceremony, a kama sutra, like two people sitting naked on a bed and not touching. The ultimate arousal, not touching, not caring. Whoever moves first loses. So when our hands did accidentally feel the skin of the other, when her scent or her breath struck me, it was trembling. It was hypnotic.

"So what are you getting for Christmas?" We were in her kitchen; she was sitting up on the counter, the window to her back, twilight around her. She spent most of our time in her kitchen. I shrugged.

"Let me put it this way. What do you *want* for Christmas?" she asked.

I thought motorcycle. But I said, "I want a tattoo."

"Is that all?"

"Yeah."

Reggie pulled on her black boots and a coat. She went to the refrigerator and took Cody's bottle of chilled vodka. "I know a place," she said. "It's on Melrose."

She cried, she drank the vodka from the bottle and cried to herself through the humming stings. I stood impatiently behind her, excited by her crazy courage, fascinated with our rebellion. I whispered, "Are you up to this?" and then watched the mystery. She took my hand and wrapped it under her chin, curiously around her throat.

"I want to go first," she'd said.

Hers was a petite, two-color rosebud in green and red, planted inches below her belly button and off-center in the crease of her abdomen and leg. As far as Reggie would hike her dress. The tattoo was highly feminine and unoriginal, the old man was a mechanic, not an artist. Thousands of women would wear his rose by the end of the California year, but it was erotic to watch it appear under the needle and to feel the pain it caused, tightening her body. Men would want to touch it, to kiss it and lick it. I remember thinking who would be the first? Lonnie or Cody? And knowing all the time, that if I asked it would be me.

Mine was a slender bird, sparrow-looking except the man gave the wings a wide spread and distinct fingers of feathers on the tips like a hawk. A confused piece of work from the beginning, the kindly expression of a sparrow on the body of a hawk. It hurt and now I sank in the chair with her behind me. I put her hand on my throat. The old man muttered around a cigarette as he worked, complaining about something, but it just seemed that after playing on Reggie's stomach, putting a bird on my leg was a pain in the ass. In one artistic stroke he colored it black and blue and I liked that. A blue body, black wings.

We would smell like rubbing alcohol for days. I wanted to tell her that I loved her no matter what. I wanted to tell her about Lonnie and me and the crime. But I didn't tell her a thing.

And Jello felt the cold. She was the first to feel it, she had a quick intuition and bright black eyes that missed nothing. but she didn't understand it. We were already fucking with the TV on. And she didn't get it. It didn't take long before I found myself waiting until she was asleep, dressing quietly and slipping out. That was how things got, Jello, and I wasn't fool enough to think that she didn't hear the lock snap and the door close, no, she was laying there in the dark with her eyes open waiting for me to go. Letting me go like any ordinary fuck-an'-run, without a word of good-bye.

Jello had herself a foul-ass mood on. I could see it in the way her lips were set against each other, very thin. She picked at her fingernails with a stir stick at the far end of the bar. The jukebox hadn't played a song and it was quiet, depressing. Jello wasn't passing out any red quarters.

"What are you so mean about?" I had asked her with my first free drink, but she just moved away and left my money on the bar. It was Christmas Day. And the St. Charles Club was empty, but it was early; the misfits would be there later. The misplaced, the homeless, the familyless, the trash like me, and they would get drunk as hell tonight. And I was waiting for Lonnie with these thoughts loose in me, running over each other, free-associating mental dust devils, but I knew one thing; I was turning cold and I didn't care. I had been a guy in love with life, with each fucking second of it, snapping my fingers to it with heat. Now I worried about it. And of course, Reggie. "I got the tattoo to prove it," I said aloud, and Jello turned but misunderstood; she mixed me another drink.

Lonnie came in. He was buzzed, finger-tapping his way down the rail to me. He looked good all in black, made him look big and wide open, and he came in with energy, like his blood was just hotter than ours.

"I'm the boy!" he announced himself and that made Jello laugh.

"She won't even talk to me."

Lonnie's voice changed when he talked to me; it was suddenly purposeful, turned hard and pointed, covered as if it was rubberized in his throat. He said, "Colored girls is like that . . . but you should know." He slapped cigarettes on the bar, "Short-stickin' won't get the job done. But when they love you, baby, it's all the way through."

"Ready to go?"

"I'm buggin'. I need a drink or two." He caught my eye on him. "This is a cake walk, okay?"

"You're sure he's not home?"

"He ain't there."

My face told him I needed more.

"I know . . . I jest left 'im. Even he's got a mother an' some place to go for Christmas."

Then Teddy and Big John the Rifleman came in full of boozy cheer and Lonnie bought the first round and gave Jello a dollar to play "Easy Money" by Ricki Lee Jones on the juke. The atmosphere in the bar changed; Lonnie seemed possessed with forcing the change, while I sat like a mute foreigner on my stool. Lonnie grabbed Jello and drinks and dragged her to me. "C'mon, Ray the Face, you lookin' like a fish 'gin," laughed Lon, and it was genuine. True. He raised his glass, "You're still my job . . . you believe that," and he toasted the three of us. "Merry Christmas, motherfucker."

We drank until it was dark enough.

"Movin' into a lit'le B and E," said Lonnie as if he had been waiting for a long time for it to happen. Looking forward to it. We were still sitting in the car, parked on the cold street down from Ten Speed's house. "A lit'le B and E," he said it again. "Who's goin' in?"

"I will. You stay by the window."

"It's in a white box in the . . ."

"I know where it is."

With a stick I lifted the window over the air conditioner, balanced it against my leg, lowered it to the ground. "Ten Speed," I called twice into the house, my voice slinking out out from me, almost tickling my mouth. I climbed in the window, stepped down on the couch.

"Stay right where I can hear you," and Lonnie flattened himself against the house, watching down the driveway.

"Cool, cool," he said.

The room was patterns of deep-green darkness; I felt the nearness of furniture, never seeing more than the drowsy lines falling away to the floor. I moved in a slow sureness into the second room, called "Ten Speed," again, but didn't wait for an answer. My eyes quickly adjusted to the darkness, but watching my hand swing open the closet door I felt suddenly troubled by the thickness of the air, the grainy quality of everything, the silence like black rain I saw around me. My hearing was acute. In contrast the white box seemed to float on the closet floor.

I stopped and looked back at Lonnie's window. For a long time I did not move at all. I was paralyzed, then I started to breathe. I slid back the lid on the plastic runners; it was a large Chinese mystery box, only one way to open it, but I had watched over Ten Speed's shoulder more than once. I pulled out the laundry by handfuls, holding it in a lump between my knees. The drugs and money were at the bottom. Three one-pound Ziploc bags, clear, and the pot was deep brown and smelled good an' musty. A large plastic jar, a typed medical label from Redondo Beach Hospital, an inch of Seconals remaining in the bottom, and beside it a roll of money wrapped tight by two rubber bands. I flicked it with my thumb; the bills were small, tens, twenties. Ghetto money. I shoved it in my back pocket, stuffed the laundry back in the box. I started to be neat about it, but what the fuck was the difference? I stepped toward the window, never taking my eyes off of it, and Lonnie's head jumped in.

"Get down Ray! Down . . ." and he was gone.

I crawled to the window on my belly; there was a wind blowing in, but I heard nothing else. I rolled over, face up, listening, listening. The pulse in my neck was crazy, like a stutter, and I had to look at my chest to see that I was breathing hard; I couldn't hear it. I got weird-sleepy, closed my eyes. Heard nothing. There wasn't time for more, an angry rushing sound in the street, a car, but it was far away. Stray radio music, feet. Lonnie's head and quick laugh.

"Sorry baby . . . let's get outta' here. Hey, open your eyes, Face."

Outside, the air was thin. I handed Lon the money, started laughing. "I gotta walk," I said chuckling.

"You can't walk!"

"I have to." Head down I passed under the street light's neck and halo, yellow, pale, breathless on a stir of sexual breeze. It was like music, I was walking in the music. Salty light fell on the hunched-shouldered thief; I was laughing and couldn't seem to stop. "It's fucking Christmas," and I could not believe it.

14

The old man stares into the smoky dark glass of the night-club window. The club is a rundown bar on Lower Broadway in a block that appears deserted but for the trash at the curb. He peers in. The sign in the window reads LIVE ENTERTAINMENT NITELY. The bar looks very closed in the warm daylight, but the door is open and the old man enters quietly.

A gaunt woman with bloodshot eyes and a long skinny neck is stocking the bar with bottles of liquor and half-gallon jugs of red wine. At the far end of the bar in a circle of overhead spot lights, a thick middle-aged man reads the paper and drinks a beer with a glass of tomato juice. His ashtray is crammed with dead cigarettes and one live one. The old man is on him before he can look up from the paper.

"Good afternoon," the old man says lightly.

The man stares at him, then looks to the woman.

"You don't remember me. I came in last week an' you said I should come back sometime this week."

"Come back for what?" The man smirks, raises his hands.

"To audition. You said you would let me audition. The saxophone."

"You're joking," the woman says. "You're lookin' for a free beer, right?"

The old man turns to see her laugh, shakes his head.

"Look," the man speaks with a cigarette in the corner of his mouth, talks with guzzling sounds, "you obviously don't have the slightest fuckin' idea what goes down in here, or you wouldn't be here now with this shit." Again he raises his hands.

"Maybe I could just play something quick for you." The old man unsnaps the case, lifts out the horn.

"Toss this old fuck, will you, Rusty?"

"But you said I could . . ."

Rusty slides him a draft beer over the bar. "Drink this and consider it a piece of good luck. Then get out," she says, and forces a smile.

The man laughs, shakes his head. "Where do they come from?"

The welfare office is very, very hot, the fans only move hot air over the heads of lines of sweaty people. The old man has been waiting in one line and then moved to another for over an hour and a half. There are two officers for two hundred people, the other desks are vacant.

A black woman faints. She falls like a soft pillow but her head hits the concrete floor and her ear immediately begins to bleed. The young child with her is screaming and people rush to help her. A crowd bends in over them and the old man can see no more, but he takes advantage and moves up to be third in the long line.

His turn comes before the others return to line. He sits at the officer's desk. He is a young Spanish man with large rings of sweat under his arms and a small fan at his feet, blowing up.

"Yes?" the officer asks.

"I was hoping you could help me," starts the old man.

"What's your problem?" the young man quips quickly. Annoyed.

"I haven't received my check for almost three weeks. It was supposed to come on the twelfth."

"Can I see your tracer form?"

"I don't have . . ."

"A check tracer form," the officer snaps. "A-1063. A yellow form. Ask the information girl in the first line, the desk by the door.

"Is there some way I could . . ."

"There is nothing I can do without a yellow tracer form. Next."

The street is split in two. The grass meridian draws other old men who come to spend their afternoons, sitting on the hard park benches, playing dominoes on small tables in the shade. By now the buildings have already blocked the sun for hours, but the street is not cooled. The heat pushes through the old man's feet with each step. He stands at the crosswalk looking at the grass park meridian, he searches for his only friend, the blind man named Ricard. He is very tired, very fucking tired, but there is Ricard, under the dead tree where he has deliberately fixed newspaper sections in the empty branches over his head to shade the broken back bench that no one but a blind man would use. The old man smiles, he almost waves hello, so happy to see him that he would make a fool of himself. But he knows Ricard would make a fool of himself too. He would be happy too. The blind man has his nose slightly lifted into the air, his head jerks quickly to the old man's footsteps as if he were waiting.

"Hello, Mr. Ricard. Is it too early for a can of beer?" says the old man.

Mr. Ricard is black and badly off; he tries to keep himself clean, but his shirt is stained with spit he can't see, the zipper of his trash-can pants is broken and down. His hair is matted and he constantly scratches at the fleas he can't rid himself of. His accent is heavy West Indian.

"No, no. Hell-oo, Mr. Rayson," he calls the old man. "No, I 'ave mine right 'ere." He pulls a can from his side pocket.

"And mine right here." The old man sets down the saxophone and rests himself beside the blind man.

They sit in the shade of each other's company and drink.

"The dumb fuckin' bastards have lost my check again," says the old man after a long swallow.

"The shit flingers are there for life, man. Bah!" He turns his head toward his friend. "Is it a pretty day in the sky?"

"Not bad," says the old man. "In the sky, not bad."

15

The girl wasn't very pretty, but she was a rich little slut. And somehow knowing that her father was a wealthy doctor with an important name made doing her even better. Fucking the rich. The doctor was so good that Ray had heard his mother say, "The man's a saint . . ." but the rest of the family was damaged severely. The mother was an alcoholic who stayed in her robe all day, one son killed two kids in a crosswalk with his dad's car and the other son killed himself with a piece of rope while he was masturbating. After that no one else tried it much. And Vicki was strange herself; she would not go out with anyone from the school, not a single date that could be remembered, but she would screw without being asked twice. She liked it. She liked to give off this attitude that she was more advanced than the other kids when it came to things like sex, she was more sophisticated. But Ray knew, she liked the humiliation. And now it was his turn.

She sat in her new car at the top of Lovejoy Hill; one door was open and Vicki stretched over, put her foot on the button holding off the interior lights. Ray was away from the car, facing the bushes, urinating loudly on the hard ground. He held himself with one hand and chugged a fresh beer with the other. He was drinking scared. He looked at his dick in his hand as if waiting for a sign. It didn't look like much; he glanced over his shoulder at the darkened car, the outline of Vicki's head above the seats, then back at his dick. It sure didn't look like much. The sounds of the park at night leaped against the quiet, the air was hot and fragrant with rich cedar trees that hovered over him heavy and black, blocking the faint neon light. Mosquitoes bombed him, singing past his ears, and down the hill the last innings of Little League baseball sounded lonely and desperate. Vicki waited slumped in the car, he didn't have to look. He wanted to fuck her more than life, but he was afraid and nervous enough to pass out. He drank off the beer and swallowed it with a deep thud. His face broke a sweat from just thinking about it and he wiped his palms on his jeans, ran them through his hair, then wiped them again. She was waiting. He sensed an emergency and a sudden complete loss of balance, his body temperature rocketed. His socks felt like electric blankets. He bent to untie his tennis shoes and fell on his face, barely missing the puddle of his own piss. Out cold.

He wasn't out very long, but it was enough to make him forget where he was, and the sudden explosion of trees and bushes and black crawling sky baffled him. Vicki knelt over him with one hand on his chest, her head cocked to her shoulder like a dog that doesn't understand the command. What?

She spoke first. "Are you okay, Ray? Jesus . . ."

She seemed to tower over him, and he said nothing, fighting quickly to get his bearings.

"One minute you're wizzing in the bushes an' the next thing I look over and you're flat out on the deck," she said.

The deck? thought Ray. But he recovered, "I tripped . . ." He searched the ground with his hands for something to blame.

"It looked like you fainted."

"Fainted? Shit." he climbed to his feet. "Shit, Vicki, I was just fuckin' around."

"You look kinda pale."

"Let's get in the car, okay?"

Her new car had fold-down front seats and in no time Ray was on his back, staring out through the sun roof. He was sweating and already had the beginnings of a good boner working its way up his pocket. When Vicki opened his shirt, Ray was ready, no longer thinking. She touched his chest.

"God, Ray, you're hot."

"Fuckin'-A I am!" he howled and grabbed her with both hands.

They started necking immediately, and she was good; her mouth tasting lightly of lipstick, like oranges, her lips wide and soft. Ray opened his eyes twice to see if she was looking, but she never was. She's digging this too, he thought. He Frenched her and she jumped right into it, her tongue gouging back like a cornered, sleek varmint, attacking, and a moaning, thick *Oooouuu* came from her like wind through a cave. She stopped long enough to open the driver's door. "Here . . . you can stick your feet out," she said with experience. He laid on top of her and she felt his boner and began grinding herself into it, arching up so that his head was jammed under the arm rest and his neck pinched in sharp pain. But he didn't stop. This was it, he was sure, this was it.

They dry-humped and dry-humped. Vicking insisted on the mad smash kissing; they were afraid to let their mouths go, like this was all OK as long as they were kissing, but if their mouths separated, their bodies would have to separate too, the kind of grip-kissing that was giving Ray a sore jaw, swollen lips. And there was something else in Vicki's technique, an embarrassed pain growing inside of her, passing through her body like shivers of conscience, but the more she shivered, the more she would pull him in and the wilder her mouth would be on his, pressing, smashing so their teeth clicked together. Another long shiver and her legs would jump a little wider apart, as if she were shoving her inner conscience away, out of the car. And Ray's conscience? It was rubbing itself into a nasty scab inside his pants, his dick against the zipper like a cheese grater. But he was too gone to notice. It didn't matter who she was as long as she didn't stop. This was it. His hands moved up her thin sweater, slowly, cautiously, a thumb, then a finger, then another crawling up like a thief. She shivered and took his hand and awkwardly forced it under her bra, exposing her sweet tit, his cold-hand panic, his fingertips not knowing what to do, but just lying there while her nipple stood up under them. "*Ooooouuuu . . .*" coming from her and scaring him into peeking with one eye. He thought she was crying.

After that he was afraid to open his eyes; he could feel her looking straight at him. The little car was bouncing so violently the glove compartment flew open. Vicki slammed it closed. She took Ray in her hands and rolled him over as if she were diapering a baby. She climbed on top. And the clenched kissing was even more animal with her in control. She pressed him down in the seat with her legs. Her skirt was riding up her thighs and his hand went under it, not slowly anymore but a direct hit on the tangled lace strip of her panties, warm and damp to the touch, stiff little hairs curling out under the lace. His fingers slipped inside the matted pubic hair and Vicki's thighs flexed straight, hard, her knees locked. She pulled her hands free and unzipped his pants enough to work his hard-on out in the open. "Say you love me," she begged, "say it."

"I love you." Ray obeyed, feeling the terrible embarrassing pressure, knowing he was not going to make it. He opened his eyes, watched the whole thing with a shrug.

"Oh, God, Ray!" She had barely touched him when he shot straight up in the air, came like a squirt gun. "Oh, God . . . you got it all over my sweater!" Vicki's face was frozen with her jaw dropped open, the disgusted shock made her eyes wide and bugged. She still held his dick in one lifeless hand; with the other she dabbed at her sweater. "My God, it's all over me!" she screamed and finally released him. "You got it all over me."

"Sorry." He left the car without looking back at her. Went behind a thorny bush away from the car, still aware of the tempo of his blood, the pulsing in his ears, the metallic smell of his breath. It was still hanging limp from his jeans. And now it hurt. He eased it back inside. "Christ!" The night was suddenly so quiet.

"Ray? What are you doing out there?" she called.

"Nothin'."

"Come on. I've got to get home."

Sudden gusts of wind came up, common on summer nights by the river, and with the wind came drizzle and streaking webs of high cloud lightning. The wipers cut circles of gray mist from the windshield, a crazy wap-waap-waaping rhythm, the moving headlights shining rainbow winks of reflection off the wetness of the street, and the tires squealed as they cornered back onto Lovejoy; she was late, driving fast with the radio up. He braced a hand against the dash and watched her drive. She was pissed and looked absurd, hints of rich-girl heartache, the early stages of the road to hell, hard iron-file eyes and a zombie pout.

"Take me back to the library. I can walk from there."

"Duck. Get down." she pointed to the seat. They were driving past her house; she turned off the headlights, cut the engine, coasted on by. Other than that she said nothing and would not even glance at him. He stuck his head out the window and let the rain wash his cheeks.

His friend Toothy was waiting just outside the library door. Vicki slowed the car and Ray jumped out; he was laughing.

"Don't ask me, Toothy," he said. "It was great."

And Toothy's eyes were flecked with an awed yellow madness; he had a pencil stuck behind his ear and he motioned Ray closer with a wild waving arm. Ray could smell the sweet stick of Juicyfruit worked flavorless in his mouth.

"Got any more cigarettes, Toothy?" asked Ray.

Toothy fumbled one out, meeting Ray's drowsy liquid stare with a quick, greedy laugh, not really meaning to laugh, but getting ready to say something. Ray waited for it to come. Toothy would do almost anything for Ray; he didn't have any friends except for Ray. Neither of them were popular. Toothy was poor, he wore an old blue T-shirt and a jacket open over it. He had his books and Ray's books at his feet. The library was closed. He had waited.

"It smells doesn't it?" he said, "Like catfish . . . doesn't it."

"Yeah, kinda," laughed Ray. He stuck his fingers under Toothy's nose. "Here."

"Jesus!" Toothy batted him away. "You screwed her?"

"Sure. Everybody's screwed her, Toothy. 'cept you."

"But you could talk a dog off a meat wagon, Ray . . . I can't. I can't do it like you. I got to sneak up on them in the dark," Toothy said with a strange grin. It had stopped raining, only a lull, and they walked through town. No one was out but cars were parked at angles to the curbs, like thorns on a branch. The street lights were dull and colorless, like light through round bellies of ice. "She's got great tits, huh?"

"Great tits, hard nipples, like spoolies." said Ray. They walked on through the center of the dead town; sounds were coming from corner bars, music and voices, shouts were heard in the alleys, but they saw no one, passed no other faces than their own. The stores were closed, the gas station lights stayed on, but the pumps were locked. Toothy was talking but Ray was not listening; he stopped him with his hand. "She said the wildest thing." Ray watched Toothy's eyes hopping over his face, looking for clues. "She wanted me to tell her that I loved her, man. Isn't that wild?"

"What do you mean, Ray? You don't even know her."

"She said, 'Say you love me.' "

"No fuckin' shit!" Toothy shook his head, then suddenly he realized. "You do it?"

"Sure. If that's all she wants." Ray held up his hands.

"Why not?" answered Toothy.

The rain came again, easy summer rain, street puddles splashing and misty halos circling the globes of older street lamps lined like rows of saints' heads, rain they could throw back their heads and drink. They buttoned their books inside their jackets, the rain growing too hard to walk through, and they moved under storefront awnings and jumped puddles instead of just wading through. He looked at Toothy walking along believing he had fucked her, and why was it so cool that he believe that? And the older buildings still had sagging canvas awnings, striped red and green and white, with the rain sounding *whump, whump, whump* when it hit the cloth, rolling to a big puddle in the middle. From underneath a bulge. And Ray punched that bulge, sending a burst of water, tearing a hole, and he didn't give a fuck, thinking, If I had a car, I'd leave right now . . . right now in the rain. Toothy yelled, but he hit the awning again and again, until it ripped open as easy as a knife.

Their houses were in the row neighborhoods by the river. Toothy's came first and Ray ducked up under the front porch with him for a minute to shake off the rain. The yellow outside light popped on and jumped them a bit, but no one came out; Toothy's mother only wanted him to know that *she knew* exactly what time he got home.

"She's a fuckin' drag," he said. Toothy took a sheet of paper from his binder, handed it to Ray. "The algebra . . . you better copy it. I know he's gonna ask for it. There were a couple I couldn't get."

"Okay. Thanks. Jesus . . ."

"What?"

"Aw nothin' . . . I don't know." Ray stood there staring out at the rain with his hands in his pockets, listening all around him. He felt the defeat.

"What?" repeated Toothy.

"Nothin'. I don't know. Tomorrow, man."

He reached his own porch with a cracking split of lightning not far out on the river and a solid roll of beefy thunder; the instant of the flash he saw the whole street-long neighborhood, white-blue outlines around the houses and trees, then blackness again. A picture, he thought. He tiptoed, moved burglarlike to the front door, listening. Yeah, they were fighting again. He backed away from the door, congratulating himself on how quiet he was, and slipped as far as he could to the edge of the porch, to where he could sit down against the wooden siding without being hit by the rain. He felt his pocket for the day-old butt he had saved and lit it up. And a nastyass stale butt it was too, already smoked once and picked out of the ashtray, tasting burnt smoke. But he used the trick a kid in the band showed him for stale cigarettes, putting two dots of spit at the business end so the smoke was kinda cooled through there and it was all right. It made him drowsy, resting his wet head against the peeling white porch wood, his legs pulled in close to his chest, everything dreamy and far away, mesmerized by the rain curtain falling from the eaves, rattling the honeysuckle hedges like a shaking hand and the sound of the slop-splash. He used to hide in there, crawl behind the hedge to a hole he kicked in the latticework under the porch, and no one ever found him. He'd played the games as a kid, games where he hid and tried not to be found. ". . . they never caught me," he said to himself. The rain had turned the yard to mud and bristly tuft heads of grass; it was an ugly yard except for the tree, the cottonwood. He used to play marbles under it, a dirt circle, and Ray was thinking this: His father put six cat's-eyes in the boiling water and cooked them. "Watch . . . I'll show you a good trick. It'll really piss 'em off," he said, and Ray knew he had been drinking because he said that and because he could smell it. His mother had taught him that. But his father cooked the marbles, then put them on a tray in the freezer over night. In the morning his father had forgotten, but Ray brought them from the freezer and his father smiled and laughed out loud. He took him out under the tree, drew the circle with the toe of his shoe, and placed the frozen marbles in the center. "Now hit one." He smiled. Ray knelt and shot a regular marble, and Bam! The frozen one cracked in half. He looked up to his dad. "Put those froze marbles in the pot . . . it really pisses 'em off."

Before he knew it the cigarette was burning his fingers; a last puff and he flipped it over the rail. Washed out his mouth with a handful of rain. And it seemed to him that he had listened to these sounds of fighting and crying behind cracked doors and screened, dirty windows all of his life. The words were harsh, the expression of the words, the attack, that's what was harsh, and the crying was bitter. But now it was different. It was one-sided. It was only her voice.

Ray crept close enough to see through the crack, clean hard-edged light knifed to the floor, up to the ceiling from the shade of a corner lamp, one cone of light spreading jagged angles across the ceiling, and the other shining down on his father, like a cardboard man with his head back against the arm chair. His jacket lay across his lap and his eyes stared down at his folded hands with the boozy, moist sponginess of a drinker. Jesus, he was so old. He said nothing, lifting his innocuous stare to the window crack, and Ray pulled away not to be seen. His father was a burned man. Ray realized that some time ago, but the little shock waves still hit him across the room, the feeble hand gestures that meant "Good night, son" and "Get the hell outta here" at the same time.

And she was kickin' his ass tonight.

"Help each other?" she screamed. "You can't even help yourself. Are you ever home? Any excuse to drink and run, just drink an' run . . . with women. Isn't that right, James?" Pause. "Don't look at me as if I wasn't supposed to know. You bring the smell of their black breath to bed, *to my bed!*" She spit anger, then cried. Tireless tears from metallic eyes, not violent, but simply because there was nothing else she could do but cry. She was supposed to cry. And he remained silent, his cheekbones creased into a brutal, numb smile that he wore more and more now. Mother and father and their private sorrow, and it was easy for Ray to imagine, there was no laughter at all. Mother needed her martyrdom to fill her just as Dad needed booze and women, Ray could understand that. He only wondered what he needed to fill him?

Ray walked away from them, off the porch, out into the rain. It swirled and hummed in the warm air about him, flooded his face and soaked his clothes to the skin. Under the great cottonwood, the wind was running up from the south, eerie and murmuring, incoherent, and he fought to grasp what it was telling him, repeating crazily in his ear. The river was high and smelling strong and Ray turned his face to it and dreamed of St. Louis and beyond, Chicago and beyond, even California; in dark sunglasses he saw himself smoking cool on a corner by the ocean, not this stinking river. And he'd snap out of it just as fast, standing in the mud of his front yard, saying, Shit . . . you'll never make it, Ray. For an instant he had been gone. And even if he really didn't believe in them, his dreams became so much greater than his life.

16

Ordinary glass, that surprised me. I laid my hand flat against it, could feel the vibrations as the music hit it and I was thinking it should be thicker, it should be specially made, but it was just glass. Plain glass. Cody had chased the others from the sound booth in Studio Bee and closed the door behind them. Cody Orleans was explaining the way things were to me, he was giving me "the facts." He had cut the volume on any incoming sound and it was strange to watch them jamming in the studio and not hear the music. The kid Dancer was there on guitar and Coleman King was working his sax and Reggie was singing to herself behind a closed partition with her headset around her neck. And there were other musicians I didn't know, tuning and fucking around with each other. They were playing my music. The sheets on the stands before them all were my songs. Written by me in the bathroom in a place that seemed ages ago. And although I couldn't hear it, I could feel my music through the glass under my hand. I stared at Reggie as if I could force her to lift her head with just my will.

Cody was saying this: ". . . I didn't even know how much trouble I was in. That's the one thing about slides, they all go downhill." Cody chuckled and I half-turned to face him.

I hated his guts. His eyes were large, washed out but nervy quick, and from his forehead to his fingernails he appeared to be shining, like he was polished. Perfect teeth. An unathletic body, but lean from drugs, and those eyes, those eyes were hard to look at. He rambled on, "I was on way too much blow . . . two, three hundred a day," he gestured, shoving the palms of his hands up his nose. "I got to a point where I had to keep scarin' myself to feel anything, anything at all. I hit Big Time. Managin' three groups, two of them on tour . . . accounts began to get scrambled. Too much money. Not enough money. I got slammed. Sued. Bottomed-out. Kicked out of the biz. Like they say, it's not the End of the World, but you can see it from here."

I took my hand from the glass, balled it into a fist, cut him off cold. "What's the fuckin' point, Cody? Huh? She gave it to you, didn't she, man? She gave it to you." For an instant my eyes left his to find her through the glass in the studio. "It's not hers to give, Cody, it's mine."

"The fuckin' point is this . . . it's important that you know who I am." He spoke quickly, under control. "The moral of my story, Ray the Face, no such thing in life as a bargain. No such thing as a favor . . . everybody pays."

"Fuck you, Cody. Fuck you." I slammed my fist down on the mixing board. "She stole my fucking music and gave it to you."

"And you get paid for it. Paid more than you've ever made in your life to use it."

I pointed at Coleman King. "But I don't play it. He plays it."

"This is going to be an album. Do you understand what's going on here?" He fingered the gold chains like ruts cut into his neck. He moved to corner me in the small recording booth, he moved to get face to face. And work me. "Reggie's debut album . . . a career vehicle. If I can do it right, if I can present the best music possible, everything gets made, Ray the Face. She gets made. *You get made.*" He paused to let this sink in. "This is the most gifted music-writing I've heard in ten years. It is simply the best around. It is your music, it will always be your music. You own it. We are not about stealing." And he looked at me as if he knew, as if he knew about me and Lonnie at night. "But it needs her voice . . . you said it yourself, Ray. An' it needs his name. With Coleman King's name it will be an album reviewed all over the world. With you playing the horn it won't get done. No one will produce it. That is the facts."

I pushed myself off the wall. "No one has the right, Cody, you know it! No one has the right to give it to you, no one has the right to play it, 'cept me!"

"How many cats do you think would put their fuckin' balls in a skillet to have that man record their material?" He motioned to Coleman King through the window; he was having a beer from his gym bag. Waiting. He looked up straight at me, expressionless. Nothing personal. Just business.

Cody kept talking. "You got an ego problem, baby. That's not small change in there. An' you're taking your first shot in this biz, your first shot . . . an opportunity for a credit, name recognition on a hit record played by a legend."

"I can play it better than he can." I saw the shock in his face. "You forget one thing, the music is me, not him, not her. I can play it better than he can."

"I'm not believin' you, man," Cody turned as if he was going for the door, but he came back with a new approach. "Dig the concept, okay? Just listen, the linking of the King with Reggie with your music, the new an' the used, the young an' old, the rock 'n' roll an' crossover funk . . . you label it."

"I told you I won't tag along for the ride. Not with her or anybody. Don't you get it, Cody? I don't write for other people. I write for me."

"Then why did you go to her? *You,* Ray the Face, you took it to her. She didn't come 'round your house askin' . . ."

"I made a mistake."

"All right, asshole, all right." Cody threw up his hands. "Do some homework, man, talk to some people an' find out how it really works. You think talent always wins out. That it will come to you if you are pure of heart, if you are true to yourself." Cody laughed, a dirty laugh that gave me shivers. "It won't. That shit is dead. Now we make deals. We fight like generals, we attack our strength against their weakness. Nobody butts heads an' wins." Cody pointed to Reggie; he turned a volume control on the console so her laughing voice floated into the room. "She's a hit and you know it."

"Could be," I answered. I watched as he opened his briefcase and brought out what looked like blue-backed legal papers.

"Did you ever think about protection, Ray the Face? Did you register it? Did you copyright it?"

I could say nothing. I knew what was coming.

"Because I did."

Cody slipped the papers before me to read. The music was registered to Cody Orleans, it was titled *StreetCrime.*

"She gave you everything."

He nodded. "We don't steal, Ray. You'll get paid well." He carefully put the papers back. "I'll give you something else, something big." Now he sat down at the mixing board, fixed the creases in his pants, then folded one leg casually over the other. "I'm going to unveil her. Like a piece of art. I want her to use some of the *StreetCrime* stuff."

"What are you talking about?"

Again the laugh. "I know you hate what you see, Ray, but I think you'll get over it. I think one day you'll understand people like me, what we do, and why it's necessary." He paused, smiled as if I was going to shake his hand. When I said nothing, he continued, "The National Music Awards are next Friday at the Dorothy Chandler. After the ceremony there will be an enormous private party at Elliot Green's home in B-Hills."

"Who's he?"

"President of MCI Records. I've arranged to have Reggie perform . . . her coming-out. If you want to play, that's your chance. The world will be there. Announce yourself."

I could not believe the look on her face. She answered the door with such a sweet, mocking smile, a pricktease smile. She stole my music! Now she was fucking with me, looking me over, scolding me. I almost fell, recovered my balance. She folded her arms across her chest. I was sick, shaking with my own sickness. When I could trust my own voice, I said, "Who in the fuck do you . . ."

She took the whiskey bottle from me. I looked down at my arm and it was gone.

"You're too fucked up. You're going to hurt yourself." Reggie pulled me inside by my shirt, but I shook myself free, wheeled on her but missed badly.

"You sold yourself to 'at fancee little nigger wit' my music!"

"You're too fucked up, Ray." She backed away.

"Where the fuck is he?" I stumbled into the kitchen, bounced along the hallway, looking for Cody. I had done cocaine with Lonnie at the bar, and I never did the stuff because it made me so crazy, made me black out and keep on my feet, keep on drinking. I was roaring. My head felt incredibly large and deformed, my face felt swollen.

"He's got his own place, Face," she said behind me.

"Don't call me that! *You* don't get to call me that."

"I sent him there." Her voice was kind, forgiving. "I knew you'd come. I expected it. I was waiting."

I wanted to kill her. She had no right to look at me like that, she wouldn't even pretend. "But did you know why?" I glared at her.

For the moment Reggie seemed confused by this; it caught her off guard, she frowned and there was sudden fear.

"I came for this." I had her by the throat before she could spring away. I choked her hard with one hand under her chin and drew back a fist to kill her. To smash her. To really damage her. But I didn't hit her; she knew I wouldn't. She did nothing but close her eyes to my ugliness. I threw her violently into a wall, grabbed her and we both fell over a chair, two chairs. I ripped off her workshirt in two wrenching tears that dug into her shoulders, held her by the hair, slammed her face into my chest and tore her bra from her. Now she fought. My face rang with her slaps. I struck her in the back of the head and she broke free. I caught her in the kitchen and she was begging me.

"Take off your pants, Reggie," I said.

She was sobbing, backed against the counter. She could have defended herself, there were weapons within reach now.

"Take 'em off." She obeyed me. "Lie down on the floor ... this is where we made our best music, isn't it." I sneered at her. In moments I was naked beside her, she actually helped me undress. But her eyes were wide, watching me, sensing everything in the room. My anger had dulled, turned evil, sad, sadistic and sick. Pain was no good to me, pain was not enough. I saw her tattoo, and again I gripped her roughly by the hair. "See my tattoo?" I asked softly, and Reggie nodded. "My bird, my black 'n' blue bird. I want you to sit on it. Put your pussy on it."

She slapped me, full, stinging. I didn't feel it.

"Sit on it, Reggie . . . burn yourself on it."

She hit me again, and once again. Each time with less guts, each time she winced, not me. I did not move. I held her by the hair and she said something, but I didn't understand it; I only nodded toward my tattoo. Reggie lowered herself onto my leg, began to grind into it. "Slow," I whispered. "Grind and jump my leg like a dog." I just watched, it was someone else, not me.

"Now lick it," I ordered her. She did so without a glance at me, my skin flinched under her tongue, tried to pull away.

"What does it taste like?"

"It tastes like me," she groaned, lost. Adrift.

"It always will, Reggie. Don't you get it?" I started to weep, without pretense or restraint, lying on my back so I shook and convulsed like a drowning man pulled from a river. I arched and fought for breath. I pushed her from me as hard as I could and I cried. I had no idea where I was, or how I'd even got there.

I don't know how long it lasted, but Reggie crawled up next to me, lifted and held me, whispered to me that it was all right, everything was all right. I cried until my mouth filled with spit.

The morning was dark; I awoke confused, numb, remembering nothing. Reggie was asleep next to me, we were both naked and we were in her bedroom. My face hurt, but then everything hurt. I was blinded by the blackout, how or when or what had happened. The shock washed over me in the physical form of sweat, of heat that prickled in ridges along my body and gathered in the palms of my hands. It was close to insanity.

Reggie tensed, sat up, looking deeply into my face. "Are you all right?" she asked with a nerve in her voice.

"Yeah, I'm hot."

She disappeared into the bathroom, I heard the water running, and she came back to bed with a cold washcloth. She gently wiped my body and legs, then rinsed the cloth in fresh cold water and spread it out full on my chest. Without really knowing how it started, we were making love. I was on top of her, she was holding me. She trembled and came, and I was right behind her, exploding with fever, my sperm unnaturally hot and burning so she cried out. Then we slept.

We did this for the day; sleeping, waking, making love, then sleeping again. It was hungry, desperate. The phone rang and no one answered. The day passed in a series of troubled naps; only once I awoke and she was not there and I slept alone. Reggie continued to soothe me with the cold cloth until my temperature dropped and the strength came back into my legs. She was in the kitchen; the sounds of her making something to eat woke me. When she came into the room with two glasses of orange juice, I stood dressed by the bed. She was surprised and could not hide it, but still said nothing.

"It doesn't change anything," I said, brushing past her without meeting her black eyes. "You gave me up, Reggie." And I left with her back to me.

I knew Keeber liked to do it. On afternoons when there wasn't much business downstairs he'd sit in the upstairs landing and smoke a cigar, listening to us jam in Lonnie's room. He was doing it today. And he was thinking this: Now they're playin' the real music, not that rock 'n' roll trash. Maybe it was because he was tired or maybe because it was just one of those hours when he felt old, that his head was back against the wall and he was remembering the day his father died in New Orleans, died when Keeber was home from second grade, died on a Tuesday because that was the day they got a pint of milk for lunch. Keeber sniffed the smoke away from his nose; how in the hell did he remember that? His father was stretched out on the living room couch and someone had placed a folded American flag on his chest, one preacher played "Amazing Grace" on the upright piano and the other sang in his shirtsleeves. His face ran with sweat. Their wood shack was so crowded that the man with the saxophone played on the back porch. A neighbor passed around a pack of cigarettes. His mother was on the bed and didn't even know that he was there; the women swabbed her face with a wet washrag. He had tried to get a drink of water when the two preachers began to go crazy, pounding the piano and screaming until everyone joined them, dancing with their fists clenched above their heads. They cried and looked in terrible pain. The preacher screamed like this:

> Someone in 'is house
>   is dyin'
> Look on my darlin' boy
> Look on my church in New Orleans
> Things ain't gettin' no better
> Ah ain't gonna pray no mo'

"Nobody ever died no better'n 'is man died . . ." cried the piano-playing preacher.

"God takes the best, leaves us the rest . . ."

Amen. Amen. The sax player was still at it on the back porch, only it no longer sounded anything like "Amazing Grace."

Keeber did not understand why he was thinking so fondly of this day, why he was thinking about it at all. His father had died in a hurry, a memory with music. Keeber glanced down the hall as if turning his eyes toward our sound improved his hearing. He said this to himself: the boys are playing good today. Best in a while, the best in a long while.

I could smell his cigar out in the hallway, knew he was coming in before he reached the door.

"That's clean," he said, sticking his great head into the room, "now that's clean!"

We stopped and Lonnie waved him inside. "Hey, ol' man," he said.

"It's 'bout time you worked at it," Keeber grinned. He was feeling good today.

"We're ready, Keeb."

"Ready for what?"

"For the Big Time," cooed Lon. He ran a bass line, then slipped the guitar off, cut the power. "The agency got us a private gig after the Music Awards. It's gonna be major. We have *arrived*," laughed Lonnie.

"Is this for real?" Keeber asked me.

"Hype," I said, and looked at Lon. "An' more hype . . . but he likes it."

"Hype?" Keeber's eyes roamed over the room, noticed everything. "Used to call it bullshit. Same thing?"

I nodded.

"No vision, baby, no faith in the Hollywood machine," quipped Lonnie. He did a little shuck into the middle of the room beside Keeber. "It's the biggest thing to ever happen to us, a chance to really explode," Lonnie puffed his hands in Keeber's face, "all over some very important music people." He turned and pointed at me. "He doesn't like the setup 'cause I got there first . . . the girl an' the man." Lon was laughing now, but something had changed, very subtle, very definite. "We'll be playin' the motherfucker's music, but nooo, nooo . . . hu-uh . . . he ain't excited."

"For real?" Keeber nodded at me.

"For real."

Keeber studied us both with fat, nosey eyes, first me, then Lon, then shook his head. He pointed his cigar at the new black Fender Jazz Bass. "That piece costs money," he said, "an' befo' you two Big Timers get fired up again, Ah got deliveries."

"C'mon, Keeber. What the fuck . . ." started Lon.

Keeber said nothing, simply crooked his finger over his shoulder and walked out the door.

It didn't take long, half an hour, to stack the beer in the coolers and restock the booze in the storeroom. Tyler would do the rest; the shelf work in the store, that's what took the time. I didn't mind it as much as Lonnie; to me it felt good to be doing something physical like throwing around cases of beer. But something was wrong. Something was wrong with Keeber; I had seen him like this before, suddenly cold, brooding and gone quiet. Avoiding my eyes, suddenly he was old-fashioned and dangerous as if wounded. And yet the explosion caught me by surprise.

Keeber suddenly grabbed Lonnie by the shirt and pushed him into the wall, held him there. "Where'd you get the money?"

"Get off me!"

"Ah'll get off you when Ah feel like it. Where'd it come from?"

"What're you talkin' about? What the fuck . . ."

"Your room is full of new toys, boy, new this, new dat . . . guitars, tape decks . . . Where'd the money come from?"

"Goddamn man, ease up." Lon struggled to get free, but Keeber would not let go. When Lonnie finally gave up, Keeber sat him down on the empty boxes as if he were a little boy.

"We need this shit. We've been giggin' all over town."

"You take me for a fool." He caught Lon signaling at me. "Doan be lookin' at him. Ah'm askin' you. Doan fuck wit' me, Lon. Musicians don't have money, they have moods."

"Keeber, some of the stuff is hot, okay?" I said. "We got a deal."

"You're gonna lie to me too, huh? 'at's right, Ray? You two're up to your eyebrows in shit."

"Cody gave us money," I said, and turned away as if I didn't care if he believed me or not. "He's been advancin' us all along. He wanted those songs, I guess." I shrugged.

"Ah want to talk to this 'agent.' "

"Keeb, get the fuck off me." Lonnie tried a grin, slapped Keeber's arms playfully. "C'mon. What the fuck're you thinking about?" Keeber finally let go of him and backed slowly away. He wasn't buying any of it, but we had stopped him. Lonnie continued. "Don't go putting your foot into this shit, Keeber. Goddamnit, not now. We're right on the edge of it."

Keeber looked at me. "He's right," I said. "Not now."

He walked out without another word. Keeber had made his point. We had made a big mistake.

I locked myself in the bathroom. Everything was blue: the walls, the ceiling, the carpet, the towels, the toilet, the lights, even the mirror was tinted blue like cheap sunglasses. It was a riot. It was on the second floor, down a long, ugly corridor of the mansion, as far away from the party as I could get. I was so goddamn nervous I thought I was going to puke; it was as if my entire body was narrowing down to my stomach. I could hear it slosh. I sat down on the toilet and took my boots off. I remembered buying goldfish once, two of them that came in a plastic baggie half-full of water. That's what my stomach felt like, the goldfish baggie. I peeled out of my socks and stuffed them into the bell of the saxophone. The rented tux was too small, and I stripped most of it off, playing in just the shirt and pants, barefoot. I had to play something to take me away. I didn't like it here, didn't like the mansion or the people in it, their faces. They ran me down with their quick looks. Too fuckin' healthy, joggers, golfers. I didn't like the way Lonnie was hanging on Reggie or Cody's arm and making an asshole out of himself, pressing so hard to be included that he never would be; Lonnie, lingering at the edge of every conversation like the nervous child wondering what the adults were talking about. I hated Cody Orleans. I was careful not to touch him, be touched by him, not even his clothes. And I wanted to kill Reggie. Fuck her once more, then kill her. So I played quietly in the upstairs bathroom, nothing special, a colorless little rhythm, like a shadow on me, soft. But my mind was working and the rhythm kept going back to the violence I knew I was capable of doing. It was the beats I heard before the action, the rush right before the hit, and it was greedy, a bitch to build on the saxophone. Unpleasant. But alive. I played it in the low range and squeezed it until my throat ached and my fingers trembled on the valves. It seemed now that all the rhythms lead back to the crime, all the trails of imagination that played themselves in my head took final shape around the crime. It had become the nucleus. It was the nut.

She found me. It wasn't long enough; it seemed to me that I had just sat down, but when she knocked and called my name, I answered. Reggie was very upset, practically screaming.

"Ray, what the hell . . ."

"You look beautiful in that dress," I said.

"Look at you." She stepped into the bathroom, turned up the light. "Where are your socks?"

I pulled them from the sax, sat down and started to put them on. "I was daydreamin' . . . felt like skippin' a beat. I'm a little freaked by this fuckin' country club."

"Are you stoned?"

"A little."

"I looked all over for you, Ray. Everyone has."

I said nothing, but tried to dress slowly and not let her see how afraid I was, how the thought of that stage out by the pool terrified me. I tried to stay blank and cool. But she was the one with the jitters, with the black, impatient eyes in her face. Her smile was neurotic and a complete lie; it flashed and vanished, flashed and vanished, as if hooked to an electrical charge.

"Is it time?" I asked.

"Yes," she said, furiously biting off the word with her teeth. But that wasn't it, not the time, not the performance. She had gathered the look of confession about her, her whole presence told me that something bad was coming. I stared at her until she was ready to let it go. "Ray the Face . . ." she started, still looking at me in the mirror, backward, ". . . I don't know how to say this, so I'm just going to let it drop, okay?"

"Okay."

"Cody just cut Lonnie. He won't be playing with us tonight."

"Cut him? What're you talkin' about, cut him? This isn't a basketball team."

"Mr. Green, the producer whose party this is . . ."

"I know who he is."

"He's got another bass player here, someone he invited, his name is Akim Rashid or something like that . . . he's a kid. Green told Cody to use him. There wasn't much we could do about it."

"Then why are you apologizing?"

"You're right. I don't know why. I feel terrible about this. Maybe that's . . ."

"Where's Lon?" I cut her off.

"I don't know," she said as if she hadn't thought to look. "But he seemed to take it pretty well."

I had on my coat and I had the horn and I tried to pass

her, but she held up a hand. It shocked me when I realized she wanted me to kiss her. "I hope Green's got another sax player too. You're gonna sound flat as fuck without one," I said to her, and was already on the steps before it hit her. She came after me but it was too late.

"It's not Cody's fault," Reggie said repeatedly. "Ray, it's not . . ."

These people were rich. The crowd was filling the mansion, mingling in small groups with drinks, businessmen, record company hustlers, executives with the perfect touch of gray at their temples. No flab under their chins. Everyone was tuxed out. Club tans and thin women with big breasts and narrow, boney shoulders. Wealthy black men with cigars gathered around the pool to discuss the future of the music business. Behind them the sky fanned alive and winked with the lights of Los Angeles shifting green and white, spectacular only because of the miles they covered. Cypress trees towered in the back yard; the spotlights were all turned up into the sky. It was a low western-style mansion of glass and flying wings, so many rooms, so many doors of solid teakwood and sliding glass, so many hallways lined with expertly dressed guests greeting, cheek-kissing, patting, hugging, squeezing, grinning. I was not one of them. I was desperate and their eyes quietly followed me from room to room.

Reggie had caught up and looped her hand round my elbow as if she were trying coyly to slow me down. Reggie was very good in a difficult situation, ravishingly beautiful and unflappable; the face she presented to the crowd was accented with winks and subtle nods, flirtatious waves and smiles; she easily maintained a girlish sensuality while I dragged her down the marble halls. Some of the guests found us amusing.

"Man, you are a piece of work," I said to her. "Is there anything real about you?"

"Winning is real, you asshole," she whispered. "Beating these fuckers at their own game is real. Success, Face, that's the only revenge." I ignored her and she shut up.

Cody was at the edge of the pool drinking champagne with a handful of power people. He glanced and waved us over for introductions, but I turned my back to them and faced him, close enough for my breath to hit his face.

"Where's Lonnie?"

"Oh. I get it." He backed away. "Excuse us," he said, leading me back with him. "He's around, Ray. He understands. Do you?"

"Where is he?"

"I told you, he's around . . . free booze and food and women. He'll be fine with this set."

"You are major league, Cody." I made the sign of a hole with my hands in his face. When I walked away, he held Reggie behind.

I found him in an upstairs bedroom; the door was open. The room was empty, a light on in the ceiling panel. The closet door was ajar as if someone had just gone through the clothes. There was a dead fireplace and a red leather couch and two red leather chairs and a bed neatly made in the center of the room. Part of the roof was rolled back showing a mechanical skylight. Lonnie was rifling the second drawer of a low oriental dresser, his hands buried in socks. For long seconds he didn't see me, then he looked up and froze. Thief's eyes shining in the dark.

"You should lock the door, man," I said closing it softly.

"I thought I did." He laughed, seemed relieved. He started on the third drawer. It was no longer a matter of principle with him; he was not getting even. He accepted each circumstance that was put before him and did not reflect on how he had come to it or what it meant. I watched him go through the fourth and last drawer, staying with the dresser until he found something he could steal. Then he smoothed his tuxedo jacket in the mirror.

"Dig up, man." He smiled at me, holding two watches dangling from his fingers. "Rolex an' this little French job, gold and silver." He slipped the watches back in his pocket. "I got a coupla rings . . ."

I grabbed him by the arms. "You okay, Lon?"

"Yeah." He grinned away from me. "Fine as wine."

"Let's get outta here."

"Cool." Once more Lon checked himself in the mirror and although the atmosphere of the bedroom was rank with alarm, there was not a trace of tension in him. Outside the closed door, he stopped me, grinning. "Look, FaceMan, I'm jest boostin', you know, pay for the rental." He slid his loose hand down the tux.

"You've been smokin' shit, haven't you?" I glared into his eyes for the answer, cloudy, tiny pinholes, old, old, old junkie eyes.

"Don't start soundin' on me like some stiff." Lonnie pushed me away. "What am I supposed to do? It's your music, man. I mean, that's the bottom line, that's what we're talkin' about . . . your music."

I could say nothing. As we walked down the stairs together, Lonnie began to laugh, he waved his arms at the crowd mixing below us. "That's a great sound, man." He smiled. "High heels on marble floors. I like that. We should live like this, RayBird . . . we deserve this."

"You're right, Lon, it's a great sound." And I knew what he meant. At the bottom of the stairway, Reggie was waiting for us; he had seen her before me and now he was too cool to be believed. He kissed her gently on the neck and whispered, "Good fuckin' luck, baby." And without even the smallest curiosity toward me, without a glance, a word or a second of hesitation in his step, Lonnie floated away into the crowd like a shiny gum wrapper in a busy rain gutter. He was going quietly.

"Don't throw it away, Ray, this is a big . . ."

"Just shut up, Reggie, okay?"

Akim Rashid was blind. And Reggie was right; he was just a kid, twenty-two. Black and skinny so his head glowed like a bulb. He wore a black turtleneck and a black suit, way too big. His hands seemed to hang from his sleeves down to his knees. When Cody introduced us behind the stage, his long fingers wrapped around my hand like an octopus. He wore thick-stem sunglasses and rocked back and forth like Ray Charles. Cody took great personal pleasure in witnessing my shock, but Akim Rashid surprised me more. The first thing he said:

"I know what you're thinking. Saxophone . . . he can't read the music. I wish we had a session together, but you just go where you're goin' . . . you an' Reggie just go where you're goin' with it and I'll try to keep up . . . I'll follow you." His voice was dry and cracked, he swallowed hard. "I won't be a problem."

"I'm sure you won't," said Cody. He could not stop smiling at me. It was tough to eat all of it. But Akim was so fucking strange that Cody became nothing more than an annoyance. I focused, without wanting to, on the skinny black kid with the bulging head, noticing that he called none of us by our names, except Reggie. When he met Dancer he called him "Guitar." He called us by our instruments.

And thinking about it later, I could barely remember playing. I heard their laughter, the smalltalk at the pool, one woman's constant high giggle, the sounds of drinking, but I couldn't remember the music. And it was all a lie, the big break, my music, Reggie's showcase, all the *imagina-*

tion died when we took the stage. I had made it all up for myself, I had listened to them. Lonnie was the only one laughing now. I saw him standing off the French doors laughing with Cody Orleans, laughing with the stolen watches in his pocket and a free drink. And he was so right; once we started playing, it was just another free gig. The music was full of sadness, it seemed to me, technically performed well by a band of volunteers who stayed plain, kept within themselves, trying not to make any mistakes more than trying to make music. There was no realization, no expression of character. Reggie sounded paper-thin, her voice wavered in the gusts of wind that blew up the hill, over the bandstand. I could smell the chlorine added to the pool. No one paid any attention to me. At first there had been a ripple of polite applause, but that quickly fell to complete disregard. It was so stupid. Elliot Green sat at a large table directly in front of the stage; when two women joined him he turned his back to us. No one cared.

Lonnie caught my eye and waved to me. He moved with a group of well-dressed black men into the house; he looked just like them, his tuxedo, his smile, his walk with a drink held loosely in one hand. His cool. He was one of them. I wondered what he was thinking. About the crime? About the music? When this was over he would go back to his room over a liquor store, to stacking cases of beer. But then, so would I. He disappeared from sight. I heard Reggie's voice; she had coupled Winning and Success and Revenge all in the same breath. And I was the true failure, playing this lifeless music in the spotlight while he stole watches and rings in the shadows. And tonight we would both sleep above the liquor store. And Allie's words sailed in on Dancer's guitar line, "You're back where I met you, Ray. Doesn't that say anything?" I watched Reggie's back, watched her turn her head and clear her throat, watched her dress sway in the absurdly private dance of the performer. So you tell me, Reggie, Success and Failure, is there any difference?

Akim Rashid cocked his head at me. "We forgot the j," he said.

"The joint?"

"Yeah . . . yeah, the joint, the jazz, the jump, the joy. It's missing in action." He grinned at me, rolled his head like a puppet.

Reggie stopped to introduce two cuts from the *Street-Crime* tape. ". . . the gifted compositions of a talented song-writer and musician . . ." Me. She gave a good send-up. I was embarrassed but there was no reason to be. No one was listening. She looked at me through the angry indifference of their silence, their lack of even polite acknowledgment. She was tearful, scared.

"It doesn't matter," I whispered to her.

"Let's see if it'll fly," Akim Rashid whispered to me. His smile was like a dolphin's. Playful. His voice carried a bright simplicity.

"Okay."

One note. Then two. I closed my eyes. At first I hid the power from them; I expressed my love of the music through free-flowing chords, playing as if I were alone in the bathroom, playing in a trembling low range with raw emotion so strong the people laughed from embarrassment. I exposed them slowly to a highly personal passion. I handed them the heart of the crime, I let them know how it feels to hold a knife to another man's back. I worked to the center of the stage, rocking back on my heels, slowly beginning to build spontaneous ideas of notes into rhythms, drifting, building, drifting. It was as if I had no idea what I was doing, only that I wanted to take them with me. I wanted them to know that this was an offering. As close to beauty as I would ever be able to stand. I could not see them; I did not know that they had stopped, that they were unsure what to think. I didn't hear the band members come in one by one. I heard Rashid; his bass line evoked an immensity of compassion, an exaggerated reverence that had never come from Lonnie. Lonnie who knew the music so well was incapable of it. Rashid played the line without seeing it, without the need to see it; it felt as if his fingers were running along my spine. And when I had proved my love, I attacked. I cranked up on the sax loud and nasty, laying into them a brand of self-serving, hard, sexual rock 'n' roll that was unsophisticated to the edge of rudeness, threatening them until all they could do was move away. I was shattering the night around them.

When I finally stopped, I was alone on my knees, the horn lifted high over my head. I didn't remember getting there. Akim Rashid was still holding the bass line. Reggie came in.

She turned it out. Watching her from behind as I did, she barely seemed to move; her back swelled, her head lowered in a slowness like the long sensual blink of an eye, her shoulders jerked imperceptibly in the shadows against the overhang of still cypress. It was pure power. She glided to a finish that reminded me of the first moments of sleep, the same weightlessness.

The patio crowd stared at us, Green led them through brief applause, then they turned for the house. It was time for the video clips from the awards ceremony. We were finished. The showcase was over.

"They loved it," Cody said as he came to fetch Reggie inside with him. "Baby, they loved it. They're all music people. They don't get excited."

I sat by the pool with Rashid and had a drink. Everyone else was in the mansion. I talked to him for a long time without realizing it, about music, about friendship and women. He said very little. Once he said, "You don't have very much voice for someone who plays that big-shouldered horn like you do." And once he told me I had "a terrible imagination." He had a way of saying things I didn't expect, things that fit perfectly but in a different language from the one I was used to hearing. About the music he said, "It's all the accents. We all play the same rhythms, it's the accents that cause the embrace, the squeeze, the swingin' with a vengeance." I told him about my father and it seemed to make him restless. We shook hands and I followed him closely with my eyes as he tapped away with his walking stick. I laid out in a lawn chair and drank until people began to come out of the mansion again. I guessed the videos were over, then I called a cab and left without saying good-bye to anyone.

I knew he was there before I reached the door, but I knocked anyway. Jello's back door at three o'clock in the morning, lights were on, music was playing. It was funny because I really didn't want to go in, but I knocked again. I knew he was there. So I took a hit from the whiskey pint, slipped it back into my coat, switched the sax case to my other hand, and climbed down the steps to the alley with the feeling her eyes were watching me through the blinds. At least they had the respect not to answer the door.

I followed the sidewalk from Venice to Santa Monica, stepping around a fresh splash of rotgut wine vomit where a black-spotted cat hunched and licked at the puddle, his tail flicking contentment. In the upper storeys, brown-lit, unwashed windows shone, TVs were on even this late, the bluish-white glow stood out from the bricks like the three-o'clock-conscience eyes of boredom. My breath puffed before me like wet steam, feeling the cold come through. Two pissmarked bums of the streetnight moved away from my approach, viewing me with a professional eye and I must've looked a sight in my tuxedo, my cigarette, and my saxophone. I pause to let them see me hit the whiskey pint, getting a kick out of it for no reason. Then I capped it and held it outstretched toward them.

"Here. Take it," I said. "I don't want it." And that instant exposed a shame and sadness in me that was more corrupt, more demoralized than thirty-two years should be. And with unnerving suddenness I was helpless. Walking, washed over with a lonely sensation that made me shudder beneath the pastel rings of streetlights.

At the liquor store, I knew the graffiti by heart, Night-Owl&BlindGirl . . . Sad-doz . . . Mota 13 . . . El Lobos por vida . . . Black Rangers . . . spraypaint writers in this part of town, taggin' Keeber's wall with simple graffiti rockin' and he didn't bother to wash it off. They would only hit it again.

Through the window I could see Tyler's head ducked down behind the counter, hiding. His constant state of late-night fear, he was so sure he would die for a handful of cash. And I was remembering the first time I met Keeber, in the middle of that liquor store, like this. "Keeber, this is Ray." Lonnie introduced us.

"You're here to see 'bout the extra room, I suppose," was the first thing Keeber said.

I nodded. "We still got it, right?" Lon cut in.

"Saxophone player, huh?"

"Yes, sir, but I can do it quiet." It was a promise.

"Kin you play a little tune for me?" Keeber said seriously.

"Here?"

"Why not? Ain't nobody here but us."

I had hesitated, then after a look at Lon, pulled the sax out, fingered it and cut off into a lighthearted bop number that wasn't too bad.

"Where'd you learn that?" Keeber was smiling now, looking me over with this strange approval in his great eyes.

"My dad showed me."

"Still alive?"

"I think so."

"You in any trouble?"

"He ain't in no trouble, Keeber," Lonnie butted in.

"I'm broke as a skunk," I said.

"Broke's a condition," Keeber said. He fixed his eyes on mine, straight, hard, like it was the absolute test. "We're all guinea pigs to money. You'll get the rent." He winked. "Ever live wit' niggers before?" he asked firmly.

"Only my Uncle Harold." I grinned.

Keeber laughed loudly and gave me the house rules: "We stay up late an' we sleep late. An' about girls in the house . . . the more the better, only no Christian lovemakin' allowed in my house. If they ain't gonna yell an' scream a little, doan bring 'em up." That's what he said.

Keeber woke me in the afternoon. I was sleeping on the couch in the poker room with the rented jacket over my face; at first I couldn't find my way out of it, then I sat up and blinked at him in the doorway.

"There's a girl downstairs fo' you, FaceMan," he said, as if it bothered him to be delivering messages. "A black girl."

Reggie waited for me by the front door. When I was close enough, she took my arm and dragged me out into the bright sunlight.

I grabbed for my eyes. "Jesus . . . easy . . . easy . . . you've got shades on, I don't." I tried to back into the store, but she held me out.

"They signed me! Elliot Green signed me last night . . . in the kitchen!" She screamed, she jumped up and down like a little girl.

"Congratulations. What does that mean?" I didn't get it.

"MCI. It means MCI signed me to a record deal. Last night." And she kissed me. I fought to imagine what I smelled like to her.

"Wow."

"I tried to find you. I even looked in that stupid blue bathroom again, but you were gone. It was late, we were in the kitchen with a bunch of other MCI people, an' he just announced it. Like it was a surprise engagement or something." She kissed me again. "Ray the Face, can you believe it?"

"No."

"I know . . . I know . . . I sounded terrible last night," she bubbled.

"You sounded like shit last night," I said.

"I know! You guys did all the work." She squeezed my hand in hers, started to drag me toward the car at the curb, Cody's car. "Apparently Cody had the papers in his pocket all night. They must've set it all up before . . . from the tapes. You know how dramatic Cody is."

"Wait a minute, wait . . ."

"Face, I'll get you on this record. I don't care what I have to do. I'll kill somebody if I have to. Last night you were a monster. Everyone saw it. They were all talking about you."

I almost believed her. I wanted to. "Wait, goddamnit!" I pulled my arm from her. "What are you doing?"

"You're coming with me." She took off her sunglasses and put them on me. "I've got champagne, an empty apartment, an' I want you. I want to celebrate with you an' me . . . in bed." She paused when she saw my withdrawal. "C'mon, we've got so much to talk about. Ray, please . . ."

"Reggie. I'm happy, really, it's great news. But don't you think it's kinda strange . . . last night with Cody, today with me?"

"You don't know what goes on. You're only guessing." She whirled in a few tight circles, so happy it was infectious. "Let's go, let's go damnit! We're wasting time." She stopped to face me. "I can't believe you don't want me, Ray. I know you do."

"Let me brush my teeth," I said.

"No," she answered. And we were in the car.

And across town I couldn't see it, I couldn't hear it, but it was going down like this:

Lonnie was still in his crumpled rented tux; he stood silently in Ten Speed's back bedroom. Ten Speed tried on the watch. It was 18-karat gold with a French name scrolled across its face. He liked it and smiled wide.

"How much you want for it?"

"I want to off all of it, the rings too."

"I didn't know you were into this kinda shit, Lon." Ten Speed studied Lonnie carefully; an idea had planted itself in his head and he was looking for truth in Lonnie's face. But it was as impassive as blackened brick.

"I'm not. I'm not . . . this is a fluke." Lonnie paced Ten Speed's apartment, suddenly thinking maybe this wasn't such a good idea.

"Where'd you get it?" He tried on the rings but they were too small. Lonnie didn't answer. "Okay, never mind that shit. I'm not really a fence, Lonnie, an you're not really into this shit." A quick laugh. "But leave it; I'll see what I can get for it." He admired the watch on his wrist. "The watch is nice. Sure you want to get rid of it?"

It wasn't like Jello to cry and she didn't do much of it now, not by a woman's standards; she cried like a losing athlete, enough to wet her cheeks and bow her head. But it shocked me. I didn't know how much of my life she knew or was only guessing, but she handed me Lonnie's note and the message was clear enough. Meet me for the action. I hadn't seen him. I was waiting now, alone with Jello at the St. Charles.

"You're up to some shit."

"No, Jello, I'm not."

"You got somethin' else," she said between her hands.

"I got nothing. What'd you got, hmmm?"

Lonnie showed like a sudden blast in the doorway. He was late, but I didn't care. I wasn't going. He was high. He was so high I couldn't look at him.

"Nobody at the St. Charles tonight," he said, inspecting himself in the back-bar mirror.

"It's the weather," said Jello.

"Whether to do it or not to do it." Lonnie pointed a long finger at her about tit-high, ". . . an' you know the answer to that one."

She gave him the breeze.

"You ready? Ah got one picked."

"I'm not goin'."

"Yeah you are. One more."

"Lon, we don't need to do this shit anymore, man."

"Wrong. You don't need it. Ah do."

"Then do it. I'm not goin'."

"You dick motherfucker.

"Lonnie, it's over, man. Listen to me!"

"That's why I'm doin' it, baby. I did listen to you!" Lonnie unfolded himself from the barstool, stood very straight. "Everybody knows about me. About us . . . an' Reggie an' Jello knows . . . an' Cody an' all them motherfuckers. Everybody knows, Ray the Face. I put our shit in the street like a fool didn't know any better. Ah'm goin'," he said.

And I could hear the lip-smacking sound of fear in my ears, all wrong, like the clang of iron, mad shrieks, the black murmur of a million lips. Lonnie took steps and I caught his arm, squeezing it like I was trying to count all the muscles one by one.

"Get off me." He took my arm and cracked it against the bar. "Ah'm gonna take you out . . . Ah'm gonna hurt you, goddamnit!"

Jello screamed something we didn't hear, maybe it wasn't words. He slapped my head and I heard the door shut. There was a stir, a short, nervous stir, a glance, a breathless silence, and I was sinking, sure; above me was a sharp rim of horizon. I finally looked and saw Jello wiping her eyes with a bar towel and I went out after him.

The rain was fearless and wild, dark. I caught Lonnie in the parking lot and took a swing at him from behind, but missed and hit him high in the back. He spun on his heels like the Four Tops and hit me. Hit me so hard that I was sitting in a big puddle with blood in my mouth. And Lon stood over me, not sure what to do next. He helped me up and we got into the car together. *To go do it.* "Fuck them people," he said, "they ain't helpin'."

Lonnie's pick was a good one, old Los Angeles, way downtown by USC, a neighborhood of worn faces and whispering walks on the pavement, of buildings sealed with iron bars and locks, windows of suffering dull light and drunk, empty looks. The tenements were open, the lights in the hallways knocked out and not replaced, the corner lot was rubble, bricks, fragments of tin, foundation-slab concrete and jutting, rusted spears of rebarb. By evening the shopkeepers were closing up.

It was like being parked on a moonscape, sitting in Lonnie's car listening to old Wilson Pickett on the radio, smoking butts like they were good. I flinched to the smothered cries and street hisses that turned in the night behind me, above me, around me. I was hemmed in with loss and human time close to running out, with violence slashing through the poverty where these people lived, where they hung their old coats and put water on to boil, where they slept and filled their lungs with dust from the floor above. No love night. No love night. I held a napkin to my mouth; the bleeding had stopped. The wind brushed my hair through the car window. The alleys down here were narrow, lined with skinny shapes and dying, impatient sounds.

Lonnie had picked a good one. The little store was called Han's Market.

"Lon, it's a liquor store, man."

"That's the irony, RayBird. Wouldn't Keeber just shit."

I was silent, pressing myself low in the seat

"It's a little Chinese guy," continued Lonnie, his eyes pinched to white needles in the darkness beside me. "He's runnin' late tonight . . . parks his car on the side of that project there, the one with the gangster whitewalls."

I looked and saw the car slanted at an angle to the trick wall. One side of the car fell under the fringe of gray streetlight, the other disappeared in shadow. I could see nothing beyond that. The beer sign was still lit in the front window of Han's. The place looked like it had been hit before, and suddenly I heard a scream from down the block, and rain hitting the roof of Lonnie's car. But all I could think was this: There's no music in it, there's no rhythm anymore, not one beat. And I thought very hard about this in the seconds waiting in Lon's car. I tried laughing, but there was holes in it and I stopped. I heard my own voice. At one time there had been rhythm in the crime, side by side, keeping time, ticking off with me; there was music in everything, equal measures of terror and beauty in everything. Now it was only terror.

Lonnie's voice was harsh in his mouth. "Jesus, that wind came up in a motherfuckin' hurry." He rolled up his window.

"This is no good in the rain like this."

"It's better. People'll close their fuckin' windows." Lonnie nodded to the building. He brought Keeber's gun out. He pointed it at me, popped out the cylinder, rolled it in his fingers.

"Is that loaded?" But he didn't answer. "Lon, is that goddamn gun loaded, man?"

"Did you ever fuck her, Ray the Face?" Lonnie waved the pistol in vague circles between us. "Huh? Did you?"

"No, man. NO! Jesusss . . . what are you asking?"

"You wouldn't lie about it?"

"No. Lon, what're you doin'?"

Lonnie held himself very quiet, his lips fluttered as if he wanted to speak, but did not. I could hear the breath exhaling slowly from him.

"Let's get out of here, Lon. C'mon, man. Now. Start the damn car."

He turned. Too late. It was too late. It was in his face and I plainly saw it; he wanted to go, but it was too late. The beer light went out in Han's window. He pulled himself forward with the steering wheel, rubbed a clear spot in the windshield fog. "Hit the radio," Lonnie said.

I squinted through the rectangle of rain. I could see Han's Market go dark. I shivered, felt the gooseflesh run the length of my legs, and when I looked up again the rain hushed around a short man struggling to pull the gate across the front of his liquor store.

"Let's jump in," said Lon, his door open.

"I'm not goin'."

He held the gun in his hand, he gave me an odd frown, then flipped me the finger. "Fuck you . . ."

"You're on your own. I'm not goin'."

"Drive." He swung out, slipped his long body into the rain.

He was instantly gone in the sheet of rain. I couldn't find him. I opened the door and stood behind it. I had to follow. But I fell in the street. I cut my hand on a broken curve of glass. I tripped and fell and kneeled there in the middle of the street studying the palm of my hand. My hair was wet, in my face, I felt completely insane. Spectral whiteness burst reckless above me, lightning laying the street open at once like a razor sound, and in the flash I saw a question mark of blood in my hand. The thunder cracked and hammered at me, so fierce and abrupt I tried to duck under it; I cleared my eyes and the sky flared once more, and there, in the empty lot ahead of me, Lonnie was down too. Lonnie had fallen too.

"You picked a good one, Slick," I chuckled to myself, and standing I could barely make out the figure of Han running from his car, running on short Chinese legs, running like a goose in the snow. He glanced back over his shoulder and vanished in the alley behind his store.

We had to get away from there, we had to move before that fucking Pork could get to his phone. But Lonnie was still down when I got to him, twisted over broken bits, his hands flapping at the air beside his head. His face was turning wet and black with blood, the rain washed it down his neck and pooled it in the cups of his ears. I took his hand and Lonnie screamed. He tried to say something through the sobs, and spitting thin blood, tried to say it over and over again, but I could not understand. I had begun to cry. I covered Lonnie with my body to keep the rain from smashing into his face. But Lonnie pitched and twisted and rolled in pain, throwing his arms and legs in a hoarse breath and I whispered to him, fought to keep him still, held his jaw in my hands.

"Lon, Lon, oh, man, oh, man, Lonnie." I gripped his hand but Lonnie tore free.

And then he stopped. He rested on his side in a puddle of dusty brick water and stopped moving. His hand splayed upside down between his knees. I sat beside him and fixed on that hand. I had seen Lonnie sleep like that when he was drunk, his hand between his knees to cushion the bone against bone. I sat there and heard the silence return, the silence of night lifetime, and then the rain came back and I listened to it hitting my collar; it had eased to something hazy and gentle, plops flattened on the mud. I heard voices and a window grunting open and thunder thudding dull and weak in the distance.

I dragged Lonnie with my hands under his armpits. I slipped off and his body would droop off to one side, then the other; I balanced him against my knees and regained my grip and dragged him through the lot. Lonnie lost a shoe, his socks filled with mud and debris, trash stuck to his clothes. His shirt was coated with dark blood to the waist. I tried once to carry him, but he was too heavy to lift from the ground, so I pulled him backward to the sidewalk and propped Lonnie against a discarded bathroom sink. I brought the car to him and left it running while I hefted him into the backseat, pushing my shoulder against Lonnie's chest like a tackling dummy, bracing my heels on the broken curb and pushing him in. Lonnie rolled onto the floor and I pulled at him, but in the end left him there. I drove away without turning on the headlights or thinking my friend was dead.

17

The car was in the center row, deep in the hospital parking lot, Lonnie's car. The mercury lamps hummed and the traffic was constant, the sirens careened around the corners and wound down in front of the emergency entrance. The lot was full in the middle of the night. I hid on the floor in the backseat, I busied myself for a long time wiping Lonnie's blood because I could not stop myself from seeing it, and I could not stand to see it, my shirt and blue jeans were smeared with it. The sticky spot on the floor mat would not come out, so I covered it with my foot to keep from seeing it. In time I began to think about the police and what was going to happen; I was going to jail, but it was unimportant until I knew about Lonnie. I peeked over the seat, the rain had stopped, nurses and janitors were all I could make out, coming and going, the crowd in street clothes was gone from the doors. I was too afraid to smoke, so I just sucked on an unlit cigarette and kept my head down. I had a hard cramp in the kidneys, but I didn't move, or try to twist away, the pain wasn't hurt; it was my attention point, my alertness and I recognized it. It didn't hurt like pain was supposed to hurt and I wanted it. I had no way of guessing how long it stayed like that, the pain in my back, the foot covering the blood on the floor, the sound of the cigarette and the images of jail and his death; the time had been sold and I didn't own it anymore. The night sky was the same low tone and did not change color. Nothing was getting closer. Or farther away. I slept.

Keeber woke me, Keeber's steps coming across the lot toward the car woke me, and I peeked over the seat and it was Keeber. He fell into the front seat and gripped his massive hands into fists around the steering wheel, then laid his head down on his fists. His voice seemed starved for air, but the words were slow and clear.

"He's not gonna die," Keeber said. "He's got a bullet in his head, but they can get it. They said they can get it, an' they're operating now. Right now."

"I didn't know he was shot. I didn't even hear it go off," I began. "I cut my hand and I was looking . . ." I stopped without finishing.

"Crushed his cheek." Keeber didn't look at me. "They don't know about you yet, but they'll find out. They found *my* gun. They think that Ah brought him in, that he hung on long enough to get home. They doan believe it. The cops doan believe it."

"He's gonna live, Keeber?"

"What were you doin', Ray?" he cried, and his head came up like a gravestone. "What did you think it was?"

I would not answer.

"Sit up here," Keeber shouted. "Get off the floor." And I crawled onto the backseat behind the man. I could say nothing. "I'm sorry, Keeber" would not come.

"How long?" Keeber adjusted the mirror to see my face. "Ah want some answers," he said.

"A few months."

"What did you think it was! Robbin' people for a few months!"

"We just . . . Keeber, I know it was wrong. We just wanted to make music, tryin' to support the music."

"You was robbin' liquor stores!" Keeber squeezed a fist at me. "You was robbin' . . ." and he broke down and cried. His sorrow was deep and it howled from his chest, trembled, shrieked with everything he possessed in the world. He beat the wheel and it snapped in his hands. "All the time, it was all lies you told to me, about sellin' songs. 'Bout makin' records. The money you gave to me. It was all lies."

"Yes," I said, holding my arms ready for Keeber to turn on me. The passion was greater than any I had ever known, and it frightened me to be in it, to be so deep in it.

"We didn't know what it was, Keeber. I didn't know," I said. "Can I see him?"

"No."

"Please, you can take me in."

"No way."

"Keeber, I gotta see him."

"You gotta get outta L.A." Keeber twisted me by the shirt, pulled me forward on the seat until I could smell the stale breath of troubles. "You can't stop." Keeber stuffed the bills in my pocket, a flat fold of money. It was a service; his fingers were cold, he nodded without meaning, forcing himself to ignore the plea on my face, the upside-down of my face.

"What are you doing?"

"News, boy." He released my hand. "They'll be lookin' to jail you. Ah guess you got a day."

"Keeber, I . . ."

"Lonnie's enough. One is enough." Keeber opened the door slowly and swung his legs out. He was staring at his shoes. "Now doan push me anymo' than you have. Ah doan

know you anymo'. You woan be home when Ah get there."
He squeezed my arm. "Doan stop or try an' come back," he
said. Keeber touched his eyes, standing in the parking lot,
touched his eyes twice like it was once for each boy and he
walked back to the hospital doors. He left the door open
and I never moved to close it; in this numb strange night
the shallow bowl light didn't come on inside the car. Lonnie had taped the button down.

And I ran.

I called Reggie from Keeber's store, my bags were packed.
I was shocked that I owned nothing; a duffel bag crammed
hard with dirty clothes, a suitcase filled with music and
shoes, and the saxophone zipped in its case and wrapped
with my winter jacket. I felt the affection for these things
waiting for me on the floor at my feet, they were ready for
the fast move. Anywhere at all. And yet I found embarrassment in nothing to store, nothing to give away, nothing
characteristic to leave behind. It didn't matter. I cleared my
throat, nearly sick to my stomach, my vision cloudy with
undistinguished anger, pale with pumping fear aroused as I
heard the siren coming; her phone was ringing.

The machine answered. "I've gone out for the night.
Please leave your name and a number where you may be
reached. Or call tomorrow at the Orleans Talent Agency.
Thanks."

The ambulance rocketed by, the siren and lights echoed
off the liquor store windows, and Tyler pressed his face like
any boy in the street would. I left no message.

"Hey, RayBird, where you goin', man?" Tyler turned toward me. Slid back behind the counter.

"Ah got a gig."

"No shit." Tyler held his hand out to be slapped five.

"I . . . I gotta be in San Diego by morning," I told him.

"Well, keep-on, keep-on." Tyler flipped a good-bye, but he
didn't know.

The walk was long but it went by quickly; the traffic beside me was flying, the sounds shifted constantly out of tune with my fast stride, the sudden bursts of music were heard as drowsy winks in my ears, the rough gunfire of human voices was no more important than a smoker's cough or squawks over the radio. I heard everything in the distance, drank in the street, and this night and the warm air pushed against me so I cut through it like a drumbeat caught in the center of my own urgent step, imagining my family, trying to remember their faces, their soft voices. I came to Jello's back door as something of a surprise, as if I had thought of going to her and now I was here; I was sweating so that the drips ran to my elbow. I set the bags by her door and knocked, twice, three times, four.

"Jello," I whispered. I wanted a place to spend the night.

She opened the door on the chain. "You happy now?" she said. Her face was tight with anger. Jello bulled her neck, bared her teeth. "You . . . you got him killed . . . he told me it was all your big idea. Why, Ray? Why does the poor black man always pay for the whites? Why is he shot in the head an' not you . . ."

"He's not dead."

She didn't hear me. "Doan come around 'ere. Who in the fuck you think you are? You come 'round 'ere again I'll turn you in. I'll do it myself." Jello slammed the door.

But I had tried to stop him too, Jello. You saw him, you know he was pressing it, not me, I wanted to stop. I wasn't responsible . . . Lonnie wouldn't quit, Lonnie brought the gun, Jello, not me. My fist was poised over her door, but I never knocked because as badly as I wanted to tell her, what would be the difference? She was right, he was dead.

I took a cab to Reggie. Cody was there waiting for me.

"Is Reggie here, Cody?"

"Look, I'm going to make this brief. Neither Reggie nor I can afford to get involved in this."

"You know what happened?"

"Yeah. Some woman named Jello called and then I called the hospital."

"How is he?"

"On the table still. That's all they would tell me." Cody stepped out and searched nervously up and down the street. "Now I know where the titles come from." He smirked. *"StreetCrime."*

"Cody, I need help."

"Yeah. You do. To me, I'd say you have two choices: Run or turn yourself in."

"But they don't know about me yet."

"Yet. The key word, Ray, yet." He blocked the apartment door with his body. I wasn't getting in. "We've got too much to lose. We can't help. We can't even know you," he said.

"Can I see Reggie?"

"No."

"You can't stop me."

"I can. All I gotta do is pick up a phone."

"I just want to stay the night, that's all Cody, one fucking night."

He reached into his pocket and handed me a hundred dollars in two fifties. "It's all I have on me . . . take it. An' take this advice. Run. Run. Now. Tonight. Get outta L.A. fast."

"You'd like that. For me to just vanish . . . no competition for Reggie."

"There will always be competition for Reggie. If not you, the next, and the next." He cut me off, smiling now, confident. "I'm not concerned."

"And my music?"

"Yeah, the music. You know, Ray, I couldn't help but to speculate how it would play in the trades . . . I mean, if you're caught. The brilliant songwriter and the mugger, the dual life, writing powerful music about the dark side, music that he lived. It's great hype. Could sell records, could backfire." I watched him so casually weighing the possibilities of my life. Lonnie was on the table, they were digging a bullet from his head, and Cody was scheming a way to turn it all into increased record sales for Reggie and himself. I wanted to hit him, hit his face; the urge was hot, flying quickly to the surface like tortured pressure released in an instant. But I had no more violence in me, at least not at the moment. It was drained, dry.

"Let me see her, Cody." I tried to push past, but he stopped me.

"No, Ray, you'll only hurt her, she's just getting started. Do the right thing, Ray." He handed me a folded piece of paper; there was a name and a number. "This is the name of an old friend in New York. You can reach me through him and we can set up the royalties, if there are any. No other way, just through him. I won't talk to you directly." Cody backed inside and closed the door.

There would be no royalty checks, hell, even I knew that.

There was no one left but Allie. Allie! And I began the long walk back to Santa Monica, rehearsing what I would say to her, what I could say to convince her. But then Allie would see it. She knew me. I could tell her that Lonnie had been hurt badly . . . I would have to tell her the truth. That, more than anything in the world I needed a place to sit and think. Just one night. Just one night to rest in the kitchen that I saw so quickly in my mind's eye. Allie, please, just one night, a place to stay until the night was over and I could recover. Then you will never see me again. That would work. She could not turn me down. We had spent too much time together for that. Allie was not that kind of person.

I reached the apartment building and climbed the four floors, feeling very tired but unexpectedly relieved. I didn't know why I had not thought of Allie before this; she was

the one, the logical one when there was nowhere left to run.
She had always been there! And even now with the love
dead, she would help me understand what I must do. What
was the right thing to do. I rang the buzzer and it sounded
so familiar I chuckled.

I buzzed again.

"Who the hell is that?" A man's angry voice.

"My name is Ray. Look, I'm an old friend of Allies an' I
really need to . . ."

"She don't live here anymore."

"She moved?" I laid into the door. "Aw, cut the bullshit,
it hasn't been that long. Tell her I'm not gonna cause any
trouble. I need her."

"I'm not gonna say it again. She don't live here, man."

"That can't be right. Where'd she go?"

"Get the fuck away from the door."

"But where did she go? I'm serious. I . . . I . . ."

"I'm calling the cops, man. You hear me? I'm callin' the
cops.

And I could hear his footsteps shuffling away from the
door.

18

The river simplified our lives. It always remained in our noses, lingered deep in our ears, drew us to it for our recreation in the summer, and pushed us away in fear during the spring. Its tranquillity saved us from madness. Dusk, after our dinner, Georgia and I sitting in the backseat eating two-scoop ice creams, Dad parked the car along the River Road and we climbed onto the hood, our backs up against the cool windshield, hours like this watching the barges pass through the Alton locks. Next to the bridge. Three baseball diamonds there for the Little League I never played, but that's where the ballparks were and the picnic grounds and the gazebo and the miniature golf course. By the river. Dad smoked cigarettes and drank bottles of Falstaff in his white T-shirt and Loafers. Mother always found someone, in another parked car or propped up on the rocks, wives to talk to. People stayed past the first fireflies, white above the north side of the locks, Negro below the south side, a muddied area in between where the public bathrooms were and we could buy slush cones, lime or cherry or grape. Everyone stayed until the mosquitoes swarmed up from the banks. We left then. The white people left then. I could never understand how the blacks could stay and we couldn't take it.

"Skeeters don't penetrate their skin," men would say as if they really believed it. "Their beaks just break right off."

I didn't fall for that shit.

Dad was going to teach me how to swim. I don't remember how old I was the first time. I remember his trunks, baggy, plaid swimming trunks, and his body was white as a catfish belly, except for his arms, his hair greasy black with fresh comb tracks like deep corduroy, and a Lucky Strike in his mouth up until the second we hit the water. God, his legs were skinny and white, big pink toes and blue bubbles of veins behind the knees. "Knees like smuggling walnuts." He laughed.

I stood at the end of the docks, the old fishing docks no one used anymore, big-headed nails working themselves back up through the wood, rust holes where bolts once tied pilings to the floaters, yards of nylon fishing line wrapped around them, lead sinkers fixed on the line like rosary beads, the water moving fast beneath the boards. I had on my cutoffs. The water smelled of muddy sleep, shallow and dark brown. I reached down, unable to see my hand disappear below the surface. There wasn't any wind at all.

"James, I don't like this. There's snakes in this river." Mother in an old blue dress, hands in her pockets, stood in the middle of the dirt road. By the car.

"C'mon, Mom. Snakes!!!" He was half-running down toward me. "We're not afraid of a few snakes, are we?"

"But look at the water," she insisted, waving now, one hand, then both. "It's all brown. And ugly."

"I'll be right with him. Just drive the car down to the fork and wait for us. Won't be long. The current's strong today."

"James, I don't think . . ."

"Are you ready, Buster?" he said to me, lifting me into his arms. Hold on to my neck. Here we go!!"

I yelled. The water rushed in my mouth, stinking, foul, Mississippi carp water. I swallowed and choked it back up, burning through my nose, tasting the dirt of it, the spit and urine, the miles and miles of dead life of it. I gave up the instant it takes to go under, faster than the sinking weight of my head, the swirl of dark-brown slow motion in my eyes, popping open as if hooked to my mouth, feet first going down. But Dad held me up. Fished my face above the water, held me tightly until the coughing stopped.

"Don't drink the whole thing," he said. "It's easier with your mouth closed." I could see how fast we were moving; it was unnecessary to swim, just stay afloat, don't get too close to the rocks, the current spun us, face to face. I held Dad around the neck, my legs in a death grip at his waist, not exactly the way he had planned it. I did not want him to see the fear in my face. I tried to smile and laugh with him, but I couldn't. We drifted in tight wailing circles for half a mile. The river forked at a sandbar extending from the bank. He carried me up the rocks through the broken glass of beer bottles.

Mom dried me off. She wrapped the towel around my shoulders.

"I'm not cold," I told her.

"Oh, hell. He did great, Elaine. Jesus, he's a strong little bugger." He lied. I did awful. He smoked and drove us back up the river road. "Ray'll be doin' solo in no time."

The second time was no better; it seemed longer than the first, and my resistance did not ease off, it became worse, more unimportant. To try and not get it. But I kept my mouth shut.

Dad's patience was less cheerful, smoking a weary cigarette he said nothing in the car. Mother wrapped the towel around my shoulders and I left it there.

But the third time wasn't as bad. And the fourth time it

was exciting, egging danger on into dogpaddling fun, swallowing a mouthful here and there, but who cared? And the fifth time I jumped from the dock alone. And the sixth time he let go of me.

19

The last time I had eaten was Las Vegas. Breakfast stop. Half a country away. Everybody off the bus. A cold place at five-thirty. I had walked slowly down the street a block, no police cars, to the Lady Luck Casino for a breakfast of eggs, bacon, toast, coffee, and juice. Seventy-nine cents. Dirty-faced bums stumbled in for cheap one-dollar begged breakfast; they split the tray and two big paper cups of wine. The girl behind the counter looked Vietnamese with sad, rubbed eyes and a puckered mouth; one look made me believe that America was not the answer for her. A scabbered old man, his shirttail hanging out to cover the holes in his pants, was trying to bum change in the casino; they throw him out before he can get to me. Two young kids smoked cigarettes by the slot machines, couldn't be more than thirteen, fourteen, looking high in the five-thirty morning; they throw them out too. A sick old man was asleep on the table next to me, his hands were twisted sculpture, folded, like Joshua tree trunks with thick, hardened veins running through them. No one bothered him. Six hours from L.A. and I was still too scared to eat. The eggs had been too dry to swallow. I watched the room around me and drank coffee laced with thin whiskey. The

little crap table was going, a tired-eyed black, Wilbur name
tag on a red house vest, dull gold front tooth like a bullet
casing in his smile, had raked the chips quickly and called
the numbers like he was at home talking to his cat. There
were not many players, but still more than I would have
guessed. Two old off-duty maids playing dollar chips and
when they throw, Wilbur called, "Sweetness, sweetness!"

I left the sax on the bus, afraid of being spotted with it,
and I was happy to see it again. I took the last seat thinking
I could hide. And keep watch out the back window through
the night. In the east, the sky was turning cloudy deep blue,
a gold peek of sun.

That was thirty-six hours ago.

I looked around in the diner on Liberty Street, middle of
the week, middle of the afternoon, and not many people
were out in this part of town, down here by the river. No
reason to be. The few faces I dared examine were Illinois,
sunburned but not tanned, working-class mouths holding
back grievances, and lips that seemed working on mental
notes, hair darker by shades than California. Their limbs
were short and their hands thick, red, and sore. Men between shifts, either on their way home or on their way in,
dirty wide-bottom jeans and black lunchbuckets, shortsleeve shirts and cigarettes in their pockets. The TV was on.
But I was hungry and I ate well, chicken and mashed
potatoes and brown gravy, whitebread rolls. I was just
happy to be breathing again, not to feel the pain in my
chest. For a long while I thought I was having a heart
attack. Cramped over in the rear of the bus, the headlights
of a passing car lit up the blue Iowa road sign, my heart was
swelling in my chest. Oh, God, oh, God. I cupped a hand
over it, feeling the bulging with my fingers, thumping
wildly into my armpit so that my shirt moved with each
pulse. I remembered an Act of Contrition and fired off Hail
Marys.

Easy boy, easy. I talked to myself while the others slept on kinky necks and their cheeks made sweatspots on the seats. Release. Some way to get outta the heat. I couldn't look at myself in the restroom mirror, just lifted palmsful of warm, chemical-smelling water to my face; my eyes couldn't take it, being seen glittery in the sockets like they couldn't stay still. You're not crazy, I said. You're just hot! I was running, I could tell myself all night long that I was OK, but my heart knew I was running.

"You finished with this?" The waitress didn't wait for my answer; she took back the telephone book from the table. "You know where you're going?" she asked, mistrust open in her voice.

"Yeah, I'm all right now. Thanks."

"You want a cup of coffee? Comes with the chicken dinner."

"Okay." I tried to be friendly. "Thanks again."

But she saw my luggage when I came in. She could probably still sniff the bus fumes on me, and she looked at me as if she expected me to bolt on the check. I sat right by the front door, first booth. She didn't like that.

I laid a twenty on the table. When the coffee came, I didn't glance up at her, just kept my face turned to the window, to the noisy traffic on Liberty Street. A big red Trailways shifted gears at the stoplight and the exhaust flushed out onto the pavement like old laundry suds, and I wondered if that was my bus with a new driver and a full tank and another hunched fugitive in the back window watching over his shoulder.

I was the only customer left in the diner. I thought I could hear her coming down the sidewalk; she was speaking sharply to a child, her voice carrying but not her words, and then quickly their shadows stretched past the window. Georgia appeared in the doorway of the diner, a little girl jerked to a stop beside her.

"I don't believe this," she gasped. "I thought somebody was playin' a joke on us."

"I'm sorry I had to call you to come get me." I dropped my cigarette in the coffee cup without looking. "I didn't know where you lived."

"Ray, what are you doing back in Alton?" Georgia blushed with her own ungraciousness as she said this, but it was too late.

"I don't really know, Sis. I'm on my way east. Just kinda passing through. When I got to Chicago, I had to come home."

"Little Bit," she pulled the girl forward; her eyes were pale, but big with curiosity and shy fear. "This is your Uncle Ray. Uncle Ray, this is my youngest. We call her Little Bit, but her real name is Janey."

I reached out to shake her tiny hand, but Little Bit squeezed in behind her mother. Georgia smiled at me for the first time. She had always been a tall girl, but now she was no longer thin, her hips were wide, her shoulders were sloped down from her neck and rounded inward, and although her breasts were large enough to be immediately noticed, they were unattractive. People would call women like her big-boned. She was built like a soft man.

"You don't have to eat here," she said. "I got plenty of food at home.

"I was hungry, Georgia. I just got in."

"Where you coming from anyway? Los Angeles?"

"Can we get outta here?" I stood, gathered up my suitcase and duffel bag. Georgia handled the sax case like a dead animal was zipped inside.

"I'm tellin' ya, Dad's gonna shit his britches when he sees you." She laughed nervously. I could see she was disturbed by my sudden return

"Where is he?"

"Dad's been staying with us. He has his own house, the

old house on the River Road, remember? Remember that place?"

"The big cottonwood tree in the front yard." I grinned.

"Yes, it's still there." The little girl was restless, pulling away from Georgia, and she grabbed and held her by the neck of her dress like a leash. "But he's never there anymore."

Janey squirmed under her hold. I went to the counter and bought a Tootsie Pop and gave it to her without asking her mother. I meant it as a gift, not a bribe. Not an exchange for good behavior. Janey wouldn't meet my eyes. She watched me when I wasn't watching her.

"Better get two more of those," Georgia said as if I was trying her patience. "It's time to go."

Georgia drove a station wagon that was missing a lot of wide trim and two hubcaps; the long back windows were smeared with dirty small handprints and sticky swipes that might have been almost anything. The dog was shedding, Georgia explained; there was hair all over the car which swirled into our faces once the wagon was in motion and the windows down. There were two more kids in the backseat. Billie was three, a dark-faced, grim boy with a down-turned mouth and two broken teeth when he showed them, which was not often. His hair was cut very short, and I could trace the white line of scars atop his head. He snatched the candy from my hand, happy with himself. His mother scolded him into a thank-you, but I didn't care. Billie looked like a river kid all the way through, dirty fingernails and scabs like tree bark growing on his elbows. Sis was not a child; she was a thirteen-year-old girl with pouty cheeks and lips and an outbreak of mean, red pimples blistering her chin. Her young eyes were so clear I could see the reflection of my sunglasses in the blue iris; she was a sullen girl, pretty to a point of badness inbred. Sis and Billie were true brother and sister; Little Bit was the child of a second father, a second divorce.

"I remember when Georgia was pregnant with you, Sis, but I left Alton before you were born." Sis didn't want the Tootsie Pop, so I ate it.

"God." Sis covered her chin with her hand when she looked up at me. "Why did you *ever* come back here? I mean, after living in California."

"I'm not staying long," I said. "You going to high school next month?"

"Wood River High." Sis nodded, and she sat back to fight Billie off her lap.

"We've got a nice little house, three bedrooms, over on Grant Street." Georgia twisted to face me. "It's close to work, the kids like it."

"Is it anywhere near the river?"

"Nooo, Ray, this is a nice neighborhood." She slapped me on the arm. "Why do you ask?"

"I dunno. I just wanted to have a look at the river. I dunno why."

I sat at her kitchen table, rocked back on an aluminum chair until I rested against the wall. I could hear the wall clock ticking above my head, and I was thinking about seeing my father again. I yawned and shivered, even in the heat. Georgia had a circular fan set up on the counter so it would spray the whole room. The kitchen was messy, the house was messy. The popsicle stick basket, the macramé hangings, the magnetic faces stuck on to the refrigerator door, the knickknacks that littered the room in random, squatting uselessness everywhere I looked, all added to a lost puzzle of time and space. I was out of tune. I drank a beer and faked a smile of warm comfort, petted the dog. Georgia made cold-cut sandwiches, cutting them into squares, arranging the squares on a turkey plate with black olives and Fritos. She was preparing a surprise for Dad. The kids bashed each other about the kitchen until Georgia suddenly became aware of their combined volume.

"Sis! Sis, get the kids outta here," she yelled. "Take 'em out in the yard or somethin',"

"Mom, Andy's supposed to call any minute now. I can't."

Georgia cut her off. "Your uncle and I are trying to hold a conversation in here. Billie! Billie, you an' Little Bit go out with Sis."

"Mom, awww . . ."

"I'll come an' get you if your precious Andy calls." And Georgia winked at me to let me know I was part of this action, that she was only doing this for my benefit. Sis took the kids and slammed the back door.

"She's getting to be a real teenager," I said.

"Isn't she though." Georgia placed another beer on the table before me. She sat with a slight grunt in the chair opposite me.

"Little Bit's about as pretty as they come." I glanced at the can in my hands and imagined Keeber tossing me a beer from the store cooler.

"She's a momma's baby. That one gives me a lot of pleasure."

She stared at me, and I saw a young midwestern mother of three with no husband. I couldn't visualize any man wanting to make love with her; her touch would be heavy. I didn't recall her hair being that dark, or that ratty when I was the boy watching her practice dancing with the refrigerator door. But Georgia had her father, and she didn't need a man. She had no chance of escape, which was all I lived for.

"Ready?" she asked, and pointed at my beer.

"I'm good." I tilted forward enough to see the clock. "When's Dad get home?"

"About twenty minutes he'll be here. Depends on if he stops for a drink or not. He sometimes does. Wait until he sees you. He'll want one then." She laughed and rubbed at a spot on the table with her thick finger; she wet it with spit and rubbed it away. "Ray, where the hell were you? When Mom died, we tried like hell to find a number for you in Los Angeles. We all thought you'd be here for the funeral. You should've seen it. God."

"I didn't want to see it. That's why I wasn't here."

"Whenever you're told to be there you just run like hell the other way, right?"

"It's not that simple, Georgia. But yeah, I don't see any point in doing something I don't want to do."

"We all have to do things we don't want to do, young brother."

"I never believed that shit."

"Well, I don't care where you were. That's your business. But you should've been here, especially you." And Georgia didn't really want to fight, so she turned her head and pretended to be listening to the cries in the backyard.

"I'm beat." I stood and drained the beer. "I think I'll lie down on the couch for a minute, till he gets home."

She nodded. "Use my room if you want.

Dad was home. I heard his truck out front; there was time for me to sit up on the couch and straighten my shirt. I wiped back my hair, and he was coming through the door in the poor afternoon light.

I caught my breath.

The screen door slammed before he saw me, and I could hear Georgia's footsteps hurrying toward the living room.

"Ray! Goddamn, Ray!" He placed his lunchpail on hooks by the door as he always did; he completed the motion feeling the wall with his hand, his eyes on me. "When did you get here? BusterBoy! Goddamn!" I was standing and he hugged me, which I hadn't expected at all. He smelled of machine oil and nicotine, and he gripped my shoulders in his hard, old hands, holding me away from him. "Goddamn! Look at you!" he crowed.

"I was in the neighborhood." I felt a little funny the way he was staring at me. "Jesus, Pop, I didn't know you were still at the plant."

"Oh yeah, yeah, they got me supervisin' the Number Three Machine. I don't have to do much anymore." He had grown very lean, his whiskers were coarse and gray, his skin appeared unhealthy, too red, like a rash. He allowed Georgia to lead us into the kitchen. The sandwiches and beers were already on the table.

"Sit, sit." He gestured to me; then, "Georgia, we need somethin' to drink besides beer." His eyes jumped wide black brilliance. "Where the hell've you been?" he asked.

"I dunno. California most of the time. Playin' a lot of hands, just like you did. Movin' around. L.A., I guess."

"You know how he is, Dad. Hasn't changed a lick." Georgia put her hand on his shoulder and he patted it, a mannerism they shared unconsciously.

"I know," he said. He poured two small jelly glasses of whiskey and lifted them in a toast. "Here's to you, son."

I was quiet during dinner. Georgia managed to cover most of the old ground from high school and earlier days; she was good at putting up the old times in a light of her own making, and she was enjoying the command of this new, peculiar authority she maintained over him, a position reinforced each time one of the kids called him "grandpa." They chattered all through the meal. I thought it would be different. He wore a white V-neck T-shirt and the industrial-green work pants, and a pair of old moccasins black with age.

"Let me have a cigarette," he said to me after it was all over with and the kids were chased to another part of the

house. The TV set was loud. Little Bit was crying and
Georgia's voice could be heard calming her child.

"Hell of a family, huh?" He cocked his head, grinned.

"I just thought it would be different, Dad." He nodded,
kept the grin. "I thought you'd be fatter. I pictured you a
content old man in a room with worn rugs and soft jazz
music playing on that old hi-fi of yours." My voice mixed
pitch with a few whiskeys. I loved him.

"I never thought of myself as being old, let alone *an old
man.*" He took the bottle from the table and shuffled to the
back door as if his legs were stiff from sitting. "But I guess
I am." He thought it was funny.

We sat out on the back porch and he lit three mosquito
candles and started talking about music and playing the
jazz clubs. He remembered his past as if it were an old
movie, recalling years as separate scenes and entire bands
as individual characters; he rummaged through the drama
with hoarse laughter and shouts. Only the crickets were
louder that night.

"We never got any farther than the Cinderella Club over
in St. Louis." He paused and poured a drink and brushed
away the June bugs that were crawling up the steps. "But
damnit, that was a joint. Buster, did I ever tell you the story.
Jeez, that time I threw my horn at that big Marine."

"Yeah, Pop, you told me that one."

"He was dancing with my girl, an' when it came 'round
to my solo, I stood up and threw that bastard tenor, aimed
right at the sonofabitch. An' all I got was a bent horn." He
tilted toward some noise inside the house. "Missed 'im," he
said sadly. "Did ya bring it wit' you?"

"Yeah, in the closet."

"Go get it."

I brought the saxophone onto the porch, zipped it out of
the case; he didn't like the soft leather case, said I needed

a hard case, that some day I'd wish I'd had one. I fitted a reed and handed it over to him.

"Here, Pop, play me something like you used to."

"Used to is right." He shook his head. "No, not me. You play. I wanta hear how you sound."

"I didn't want to come back here, you know, Dad?" I said out of the blue.

"Aren't you goin' to stay? You're not, are you?"

"No. I think I'm going to New York." I hesitated, but he just rolled his neck, helped himself to another smoke. "Maybe I could work a week or two at the plant, make a little money."

"I don't think that'd be any problem. Come in with me tomorrow. We'll get you in the pits." He laughed.

"Dad, could I stay at the River Road house? Georgia said nobody's there now."

"Well, I'm there. Say, I might even spend a few days with you there. Get away from all this." He threw an arm listlessly back at the house, let it drop to his side. "It's not so hot a neighborhood now."

"It wasn't so hot a neighborhood then," I said.

"I mean, it's all black, if you mind that."

"I don't mind, Pop." I breathed into my hand, thought, God, how much you don't know about me! Stared at his face.

"What's so funny?"

"Nothin'. My best friend in L.A. was a musician, black as your old shoes."

"Yeah, well, they make the best horn players," he said in a flat, straight voice. He rubbed his face for longer than was necessary, and when he looked back at me his eyes were bloodshot and half-closed. "Say, you still got the smell in your nose?" he asked.

"What?"

"The river, that stinkin' river. Can you still smell it?"

"I guess I can."

"I think it gets stuck in the mucus up there, inside." He tapped his nose on both sides. "Can't get rid of it. Like a permanent stain. Hey, you wanna go out to the cemetery with me? See your mom's grave?"

"I dunno."

"Georgia picked out a nice spot. Got me the one next to her." He held out the backs of his hands, side by side. "New York, huh?"

"I can't give it up. Not yet."

"Well, fuck, play somethin' for me. I'll tell you if you should quit or not."

I didn't know what to play, realized I was nervous, and fingered the sweat off my lips; I eased into soft blues chords that felt like the night, a slow progression that pleased the whiskey in my blood and shot blue traces through the blackness behind my closed eyes. Halfway into some new prolonged change, I heard him stand, and stopped playing. He wobbled to his feet.

"It's good to see you again," he said. He left me and went inside.

I fished the hour of sundown. Upstream from the sandbars where the Negro families fished, they held out their stringers of catfish and carp for inspection in the last light. Gnats clouded my face and I swept them away. The river was down, dragging before me like a long summer day hitched to the sun and moon. I hadn't caught anything. I was alone, remembering these flat rocks around me as if they had names and this piece of river like I had played here before, left footprints in the mud. I turned downstream toward their sounds, looked at the St. Louis bridge

and the traffic, headlights snapping on against the night.
The black voices laughed and called through the distance,
I could hear every word they said, starting for home, pick-
ing up two mo' sixers of beer. My line floated out across a
small eddy that splintered off the main current and swirled
like ringworm on a cat's back. My bobber was red and
white, rocking gently in the dark water.

I had called Jello for the first time last night. From a pay
phone in another town. Lonnie died. "He's better off . . .
better off 'n goin' to prison," she said, and hung up. It had
taken him three months to die. He had never regained
consciousness.

I didn't see the boy come down to me over the rocks,
didn't hear him until he was standing right next to me.

"Whatcha usin'?" he asked.

"Bread balls." I pointed to an opened loaf of white bread.

"Could I have a piece of that bread?" The boy was already
reaching for it as he asked.

"Sure." I watched him fold a slice of bread in half and
take hungry bites. The boy was dirty and poor, his hands
and bare arms were rough, scratched and scabbed. He
wore a tossed-out sweater with the sleeves cut away, a pair
of filthy, checked summer pants and blue gym shorts over
them. His socks fell down into his shoes.

"I can show you somethin'," he said. "Pull in your line."
I obeyed. The boy took another slice of bread and made it
into a ball with his hands. He spit into his palms and
rubbed the bread ball until it was soggy. "The spit draws the
catfish for some reason," he said. "Can I have another
piece?"

"Where'd you learn that trick?"

"My best friend showed me." The boy saw the black case
against the rocks. "What's that?"

"That's a saxophone. You ever see one?" I handed him the

fishing pole and took out the horn. His eyes popped brightly.

"Is it gold?" The boy ran his hand over the bell.

"No."

"Why'd you bring it fishin' wit' you?"

"Well . . ." I faltered, then told him the truth. "I was going to throw it away . . . throw it in the river."

"Wow! Jesus, why?"

"Because it costs too much."

"Well, shit, stupid . . . that's why you're supposed to keep things, not throw 'em away." He slapped my arm and pointed toward the river. The bobber was dancing wildly. I had one.

"It works pretty good," the boy said, and turned back to the saxophone.

I reeled in the catfish, a big one with whiskers as long as a lobster's feelers. The hook was close up in the soft, thin part of the mouth behind the white lips, and I removed it easily, without blood, and threw the catfish back in the river. The boy watched without a word.

"Can I have it?" the boy said quietly, embarrassed.

At first I thought he meant the fish, and I turned grinning to tell him it was too late for that, but then I saw the boy's eyes and the way they fixed the glimmer of saxophone at his feet in the dark rocks.

"I mean, if you're gonna throw it away in the river . . ."

"Sure. Take it." I cast my line out once more and didn't turn around, just heard the sounds of the boy scuffling up the rocks with the case gripped under his thin, dirty arm.

He was almost to the bridge when I caught him.

"I've got to have that back," I said to him. "I'm sorry, kid. I've got to take it back."

The boy sat down in the dirt, looked at me. "I didn't think so . . ." and he moved his hands off the horn so I could take it from his lap.

20

Mr. Ricard and the old man sit drinking in the park in the middle of Lower Broadway; they are now drinking from a pint bottle of dark rum that the blind man bought across the street. The traffic roars on either side, motorcycles scream an arm's length away. And Mr. Ricard talks loud and grinning with the scattered teeth in his mouth like postcards hanging in a case.

". . . I was makin' my way to manhood, big buck in them days, movin' wit' ease." He raises the bottle. "Another short one?"

They pass the bottle and drink.

"I had my own boat. Oh, my God, the games we used to run," he says laughing crazy. "The games we used to run."

"Does it bother you, Mr. Ricard?"

"What do you mean?"

"The routine," says the old man. "The same thing every day, the same bench, the same pint bottle."

"Another short one, hmm?" and they drink, the blind man shakes a finger at him. "What color are you, man? I know you must be white to ask a question like that.

"Black as midnight in a coal mine, I am," the old man sings, and they both laugh.

"I ask you, then," the blind man swallows, "did you hear the music?"

"Yes, I would guess I did."

"Well, then?"

"You're right, of course." The old man stands. "It's almost time."

"Where are you going to work today?"

"Midtown, yeah, probably Midtown. It's Friday, isn't it?" The black man nods his head.

"Friday's a good day in Midtown."

"Too com-plee-cated," says Mr. Ricard. "Too com-pleeee-cated, man."

"Are you ready?"

The old man helps the blind man to his feet and together they make their slow way down the sidewalk. The old man stays with him while he sets up on the corner not far away. He leans back on one log into the building. It is a grocery store and he stations himself outside the exit. He hopes to get the people while they still have the change in their hands, before they have time to put it away, because Mr. Ricard knows that people hate to be inconvenienced more than they hate to give up their coins. He holds his hat in his hand so they will not have to touch him. He knows they won't like that either.

"Mr. Ricard, did you ever hear, ever in your life hear the expression 'Never Pass Up the Blind Man or the Musician'?" asks the old man. Mr. Ricard thinks for a moment.

"Is it true?" he says.

In time the old man is carrying his worn sax case through the after-work crowds on Fifth Avenue. He walks slowly. Taking his time. Feeling the effects of afternoon drinking. He finds the awning of Cartier where he has played before today, and stops. He opens his case and prepares the horn, files the stubby reed once again to make it hum for him. He wears the sax around his neck, held with a piece of clothes-

line for a strap. The sun is resting, the light shears copper
streaks on the building tops, rays striking the horn and
reflecting back into his face. Even before he plays, people
drop change into the open case. The old man, a joy and
loneliness falling in his eyes, begins the long low notes.